I0683268

Trilogy of Awareness

Heart to Heart is Where We Start

by
Robert S. Cosmar

Du Bois PA

Magic Man's Universe Publishing

ISBN# 978-0-9839320-5-5

Awareness
Copyright 2011 Robert S. Cosmar

All Rights Reserved
First Printing -- 2011

Requests for information or interviews
should be addressed to:

Robert S. Cosmar
% Magic Man's Universe
705 W. Long Ave
Du Bois, PA 15801
814-591-3363
robertcosmar@gmail.com

Printed in USA
Magic Man's Universe Publishing

This book is dedicated to my son,

David G. Cosmar

I love you very much

and I'm proud to be your father.

Healing Memory

The love I am came with me
like a shadow in my heart.
Love flows in and out
and through me,
of this love I am a part.
It whispers to my soul,
it awes and fuels my wonder,
and I seek that memory
of why I came thus under.
This is what my soul agreed:
to help souls be more aware.
Allow the healing energy
to flow from my soul into theirs.
Waiting, waiting, waiting,
I can feel and I can see
vibrations growing stronger
for the healing memory.
Something's coming.
Something wonderful
is coming.

by CJ Heck

Introduction

The stories you are about to read are special. Not so much because I wrote them, but because of the messages and energy that they contain. If you can free your mind of the clutter of your life and listen within as you read them, you will feel something waking within you.

This waking is a birthing of the realization that you have a choice in this life: to live in your mind, or to follow the whispers in your heart.

It was a privilege to receive these stories from the universe almost 20 years ago, and now it is a privilege to share them with you. I hope you feel the same energy birthing in your heart as I did when I wrote them.

Sincerely,

Robert S. Cosmar

Table of Contents I

Table of Contents II

Masters of the Park

Masters of the Park

This is the story of Walter Bohring, a man who is well-educated and well-paid for a job he dislikes. Married and divorced, his life up to this point seems to have been a series of useless steps leading nowhere. Walter Stephen Bohring has finally reached his early 50's, but he's forgotten how to live.

Walter's friends have come and gone over the years. Like most people, he's done all the trendy things that come with being twenty, thirty and then forty. He's tired of playing all of the irrelevant games and now at the age of fifty, Walter wants to regain some sort of meaning in his life. He's tired of other people telling him how he should live, places he should visit, where he should work, and even who he should be.

Despair fills most of Walter's days now. He despairs at work, because of the waste and the total lack of creativity in his job. He despairs for all the meaningless relationships he's been in that have only broken him down and left him heartbroken. He despairs for the son he left behind from his previous marriage -- even their friendship has eroded over time as a result of the painful separation. Finally, Walter Bohring despairs because he's lonely and the joy and excitement of his past has left him devoid of feeling anything at all ... or so he thought.

Walter does have one pleasure in which he indulges himself, when he can find the time. He enjoys feeding nuts to the squirrels from a bench in a city park near his high rise apartment building. It's peaceful there with walking paths carved through the precisely manicured lawn and the surrounding topiary. He's fascinated by the joy he feels when they innocently approach him to take the nuts.

Walter lives in a large western city, home to millions of people who, like himself, came there with the same dream, the dream of hitting pay dirt with the perfect job. It's a beautiful city. It has a number of parks and, like a framed watercolor, majestic mountains as a backdrop. People who live there spend all week earning money at their jobs and all weekend visiting the parks and mountains to play. Little do they know of the magic these places hold deep within. They sense the freedom and joy of the energy that's there, but few have ever experienced what Walter Bohring is about to experience.

Understand, most were merely using these places and their energy to escape mundane lives. Few knew that with very little effort, they could also find a new and abundant life -- but only if they knew where to look. Most only cared about making money and having sex and, as long as they had these in relative amounts, they were satisfied.

Walter, however, had officially passed the age of personal irresponsibility. At this point in his life, he sees through the illusion of merely living for either money or sex. What he hungers most for is days full of meaning and fun. He wants to realize a new purpose in his life, not mere pacifiers that are five days long and then wear out.

Chapter 1: The Park

It was warm and sunny in the city when Walter awoke and decided to go to the park. He went there mostly when he felt unhappy about his life and that's exactly how he felt that morning. Delores, a lady friend he cared about, used to spend a lot of time with him there.

The park had some strange healing effect on the people that went there. It was a place where children of every age came to escape the so-called "real" world. Walter and Delores had talked for hours and hours about how life seemed to lose its spontaneity and fun the older one got. They wondered if there were some magic formula, or maybe an obscure secret, to reversing the process that aging seemed to bring on.

This day was especially distressing to Walter, because Delores was leaving town and he would have to go to the park alone. He disliked the feeling of loneliness, and he didn't want to contemplate the meaning of his life alone. The fact that she might be moving away for good made the day even more unsettling. You see, Walter, like most people, was not very good at making friends. He had a few select friends, but all of them seemed to be suffering from the same defect as Walter. They were alienated from their very self and did not know anymore how to cope.

Walter sat down on the ground under the same tree where he and Delores always sat. He could see children playing in the distance on swing sets in the playground area. He laughed as he thought about his own youth when he also enjoyed such things. Why does everything have to turn into such a matter of life and death as we grow up? "Why does the play have to stop just because we grow older?" he asked out loud to no one but himself.

Walter watched two lovers strolling hand in hand down a jogging path and wondered whether they really knew the deepest meaning of their relationship. Would it last more than a month or a year? He remembered sweet moments of a similar innocence in his own life, but experience had left him with deep wounds and self-doubts about his remaining years. He had even considered suicide a couple of times, but he was afraid he would go to hell and thus had chickened out.

Walter Bohring's life had become a series of 'one day at a time' and 'one moment to the next moment'. It was as if a heavy weight was always resting on him and about to crush the life out of him. His life felt empty and he longed for change, but he didn't know how to go about it. Walter started to cry and, as the tears rolled down his wrinkled cheeks, he thought to himself, if only I could escape all of this and turn back the hands of time.

Suddenly, an idea came to Walter out of the blue. Why not go over to the playground and swing on the swings? He loved to do that as a child and now he longed to rekindle what it had felt like to be a child again. Slowly, he got up off the ground and forced his legs to move him toward the playground. Oh, he thought, cringing, I'm already beginning to feel the effects of old age on this body, as well as my heart!

When he got to the swings and sat down, a little boy came over to him and told Walter he was too old to swing on the swings. Walter smiled at the boy and told him he hoped when the boy was his age, that he wouldn't believe that either, and he hoped he would swing as long and as high as he wanted to, no matter how old he was.

From a distant memory, Walter called up the motions he had used a thousand times before. He pumped his legs and slowly began the marvelous ascent into the sky. Up, up, up, slowly at first, then higher and higher still. It was amazing! He felt happy almost at once. Tentatively, he pumped his legs even harder and it was good. It seemed the higher he went, the more he laughed.

When he was a child, he would use a neighbor's swing set to swing for hours at a time. It was all coming back to him. He could remember that, for some reason, swinging also allowed his mind to soar and he could daydream such wonderful things.

Walter was thankfully aware that he had not had so much fun in years. He wanted to see if he could go higher still, maybe even parallel with the ground! The old swing set creaked and groaned loudly as he pumped his legs, trying to gain even more speed. The higher the swing went, the bigger the smile on his face grew, as well.

Suddenly, he felt an odd jerking motion on the right side of the swing. Before he knew what was happening, Walter tumbled to the ground. The chain had snapped. Walter hit the ground with an audible THUD. His head struck the gnarled roots of a tree which stuck out of the ground near the swing set. Walter both moaned and laughed as he lay sprawled on the ground. He certainly felt ridiculous, but it had been so much fun! He was afraid to open his eyes in case someone had seen what had happened -- imagine, a man his age behaving just like a kid!

Suddenly, Walter felt dizzy and all at once, a strange feeling came over him. It didn't last very long, but he was concerned he might have a sustained a concussion for his frivolous behavior. He stayed where he was on the ground, took a series of deep breaths and clamped his eyelids closed tight.

After a few minutes, he slowly sat up and opened his eyes. His head still felt strange, but at least it didn't hurt. Then he looked around to get his bearings and, admittedly, to see if anyone had been watching. There was no one in sight. Something seemed wrong, very wrong.

As he looked around the park, he could see that everything was unusually bright and there were no people anywhere, not even the children in the playground. Where had everyone gone? But what was even more strange was that he suddenly felt better physically than he had in years. (HAD he sustained a concussion? He wondered.)

Walter got to his feet to get a better view and strained to look all around the park. Very strange. He could see no one anywhere, except for a few squirrels playing tag in the grass and a few scampering here and there in the trees. He smiled as he watched them, wishing he had brought some popcorn or nuts to offer them.

After a few minutes, he decided he probably should walk back to his apartment. He'd had a very interesting day, so far, and if he did have a concussion, he would at least be near a phone. Along the way, he walked right past where the squirrels were scampering around in the grass. In fact, at first, he didn't even notice them.

"Where're you going, Walter?" asked a voice. Walter turned quickly to see who was talking. Seeing no one, he turned himself completely around, but he could see no one anywhere. He scratched his head and then continued to walk.

"Down here, down here!" the voice called again. Confused, Walter looked down. To his surprise, one of the squirrels appeared to be waving at him. He laughed at the absurdity of it. How odd! It dawned on him again that he just might have a concussion, after all.

Again he walked on, all the while watching for signs of other people (and he admitted to himself, any other weird imaginings, like talking squirrels). Walter suddenly realized something else. There were no cars on the streets. There were no familiar sounds either, except for the squirrels chattering in their play. He was starting to worry now. What was going on?

Walter stopped and sat down in the grass next to a tree. Maybe it would be best to relax for a while. The whole situation was beginning to frighten him. A nearby squirrel scampered towards him on all fours and then sat up on his haunches staring at Walter. Again Walter felt bad that he didn't have any nuts and absentmindedly said as much to the squirrel.

"That's okay, Walter. It's time for us to give to YOU for a change." The squirrel answered.

Walter's jaw dropped and he stared at the little furry creature in wonder and amazement. The squirrel had spoken to him! He heard it, or had he? He reached up then to gingerly touch the bump on his head to see if there was blood. Or maybe, there was an unusually large knot -- there had to be SOMEthing to explain this sudden loss of sanity! But there was nothing there, except for a very small bump, he

"You're okay, Walter, but we do need to talk," spoke the squirrel again.

Now the squirrel approached Walter's left hand, the

one that was resting on the ground, and then he stopped. Deep coal-black eyes stared up at Walter, as the tiny nose twitched nervously. Then the squirrel took its paw and gently gripped Walter's index finger.

"Just relax for a minute and I'll explain to you what's happened," the squirrel said. "Understand, Walter, you're not in the same world that you knew, Walter."

Walter placed both hands over his eyes and rubbed hard at them with his fingers. He hoped by doing so, everything might return to normal, but the squirrel was still there and still smiling up at him. Walter couldn't believe his eyes or his ears. He put his hands up to his eyes again and this time, he slowly peeked through his fingers. Nothing had changed. The squirrel was still there and grinning.

"Do you intend to play hide and seek all day, Walter?" The squirrel giggled. "We have a lot to talk about and you are only wasting time."

As a reflex action, Walter started to apologize but after a moment, thought to himself, wait a minute! This is silly to be apologizing to a squirrel!

"Who ARE you?" asked Walter.

"Well, well. You CAN talk! I was beginning to think you might be a dumb animal, there for a minute." said the little creature. "My name is Angel, and I'm here to take you on a little journey."

"What kind of journey?" asked Walter incredulously.

"A journey to discover how you've been wasting your life." Angel answered.

"Wasting my life? How would YOU know if I've been wasting my life?" Walter asked.

"Because we've been watching you, Walter, and listening to your conversations ever since you first came here." Angel answered. "You're a lonely man who has forgotten how to love himself and his life. You've become like a robot that only does what it's programmed to do, and lacking the hardware to do what it wants to do. You have not given yourself permission to simply live and love it. You no longer trust in the integrity of yourself and spend way too much time thinking." Angel told him. "Shall I go on?"

"No," Walter replied sadly." I don't understand how you know these things, but that pretty much sums me up. By the way, where am I?"

"You're in a parallel universe. It runs next to yours, but on a much higher vibration. This is the vibration that we animals communicate on. That's why you can hear me." Angel grinned.

"But, how did I get here?" Walter asked, feeling totally confused.

"You were knocked unconscious by your fall from the swing, Walter. Your physical body remains in a coma back in your other world, but your consciousness is now here with me." Angel told him. "I believe that your soul felt it was time to expand your awareness so it brought you away from your mind to this place. You were killing yourself with self-judgment and criticism of all that was in your life. We're here to show you that all is as it should be. It's perfect, and Walter, you do have choices."

Against everything he believed in, Walter forced himself to listen to the squirrel. He thought about all that he was hearing. He certainly didn't understand what was happening, but he had to agree, it was time to make changes in his life. Could this be the answer to his prayers, or was it merely the onset of insanity?

Still not convinced, Walter let his anger out. "This is crazy! I don't believe in this other world you speak of and, quite frankly, this scares the shit out of me! On the other hand, I do know I have to change my life, but what the hell is going on? Who are YOU to give ME advice? My heart simply cannot take anymore disappointments!" Walter shouted.

"It's okay, Walter. We understand your doubts, your anger -- and your fears. Really, it's all right. Your heart is what we want to work on. We want to teach you how to feel again and how to reopen your heart." Angel reassured him calmly. "You will learn to play again and you'll rediscover the simple joy you felt as a child."

Walter listened to the squirrel's words. Then he smiled as he looked out over the park in front of him. Could it be? Somehow life, or maybe fate, but anyhow, *something* was giving him a second chance. How could he not do his best to at least listen and try and make the change?

"Do you know what it takes to open your heart, Walter?" Angel asked, breaking his reverie.

Walter answered blindly, "Well, I suppose it means to be nice to people."

"That's only partly true, Walter, but it entails so much more. Even more important, you have to be nice to yourself, first." Angel told him. "If you don't love

yourself, trust yourself, and believe in yourself, how can you ever be completely open and warm or caring to others?"

"I guess you can't." Walter said. "It's odd, but I had never thought of it that way before."

"Do you know what it means to love yourself, Walter? It means to accept yourself as you are, without judgment. You have to forgive yourself for your shortcomings. It means searching out what it is you love to do and then do it. It means to create for yourself a life that comes from joy and not of fear."

Angel continued without so much as a pause. "So many people in your world think that they have to be like everyone else to survive. They dishonor their own personal uniqueness by trusting their outer senses and by ignoring their innermost feelings. In other words, they don't feel as though they count.

They measure their success in dollars and cents, not by a sense of fulfillment. Little do they realize, dollars and cents will follow fulfillment." Angel told him.

"I believe that what you are saying must be true, but how do you love yourself? What does it really mean to love one's self?" Walter asked.

"To truly love yourself, it is imperative that you direct thoughts of kindness, compassion and mercy towards the self. Too many humans beat up and torture themselves because of situations that don't work out as they perceive they should." Angel explained. "They're always trying to control or maneuver things to their way of thinking. Their insecurity, or lack of inner trust, causes them to act like someone drowning. They will grab onto the first job, or person, they see to save them.

You're not meant to live in fear. You will create a meaningless life if you only do what others are doing, just to fit in and be like them." Angel continued.

"I agree with you for the most part, Angel, but doesn't a person need direction and purpose to be happy? That's something I have none of at this time." Walter told him sadly.

"Yes, Walter, but that's because you haven't discovered your heart yet. Your mind has been working overtime for such a long time seeking direction and purpose that you've ignored the most important gift you have." Angel cautioned. "Your heart is at the very center of your feelings and it's those feelings which determine how you use your energy. It is those feelings from your heart which make your life different from the lives of all others, not just your thinking. Have you ever done something just because others wanted to, but you didn't?" Angel asked.

"Yes, of course, lots of times, who hasn't? But it was because I didn't want to hurt their feelings." Walter answered.

"What about YOUR feelings, Walter? Don't your feelings matter? What would have happened, had you just said `No'?" asked Angel.

"I don't know. I suppose they probably would have gotten angry with me. Maybe I would have even lost some good friends." Walter confided.

 "Why not be your own good friend, Walter? Why not get to know and understand your feelings and see where they lead you?" Angel asked him.

Walter was getting tired and more than a little frustrated. This had been a strange and difficult day with a lot to accept! He asked Angel if he could get up and walk for awhile. Angel told him that would be fine and she would ride on his shoulder.

Walter wanted to explain. "I guess there's a lot I didn't know about myself, things that I never realized. I was so busy at work and in my marriage, always trying to make others happy, that I never asked myself whether I was happy. I always figured that I would be happy if they were, but that wasn't true."

Up ahead of them, Walter could hear the sounds of laughter. They walked towards a large fountain which was carved into the front of a huge stone monument in the center of the park. There were a lot of kids there, maybe a hundred or so. They were all playing in the water fountain and laughing uncontrollably, as children do.

Walter began to yell at them for their unruliness and disrespect of park property, but they totally ignored him. Angel tried to explain. "Walter, you have entered a different dimension here. They cannot see you or hear you, but for our purposes that is perfect. I want you to stop and observe them. Tell me, why do you think they are so happy?"

Walter went to the edge of the fountain and sat down on the low concrete wall that surrounded it. He dangled his hand in the water, enjoying the cool wet feel of it against his skin. He had to admit, it was fun observing the total childish abandon, and the joy on the faces of the kids. Seldom had he felt such innocent pleasure as an adult. It was almost as if their whole purpose in life was to have fun.

Angel hopped up beside Walter and asked him to please come back to a shade tree. She wanted to discuss what he felt and had seen. "You enjoyed that very much, didn't you Walter?" she asked him.

"I sure did. Watching them made me long for the days of my own childhood again. There was a park that I went to as a kid. My friends and I had such fun there. In fact, this place reminds me a lot of that park." Walter told her as he reminisced.

Suddenly Walter stopped, and his eyes quickly scanned the water fountain again. He had this feeling of de ja vu, of having been there before. All at once, Walter got up and ran back to the fountain. Angel didn't stop him. Excitedly, he began to study the faces of all the children splashing in the water. He let out a happy whoop when he found Tom, and then another friend, Bill, and then the same whoop when he spied Ed and his little brother, Sid.

At last, he came to the one face, the one boy he had been searching for. There he was, Walter, as a ten-year-old boy. Unwilling tears slowly overflowed his eyes as he lovingly stared at his happy young image. He remembered. This had been his tenth birthday party, the very best year of his life. He felt an overpowering desire to hug the boy, but realized he could not.

Angel scampered up beside him. "Walter, the little boy is not dead, you know. He's here," she said, pointing to Walter's chest with her paw. "He still lives right there inside you, but he's forgotten how to play and have fun. Why did the boy forget how to play, Walter?" Angel asked, studying his face.

"That fall, my parents got divorced and I remember feeling that I was to blame. I lived with my Mom and she was always concerned about making ends meet. She was consumed by it. She told me I had to get good grades so I could go to college and then get a good job. I also had to work during most of my high school years to help with paying the bills. Come to think of it, I don't think I've enjoyed life since that tenth birthday party." he confessed.

Walter hung his head reliving the sadness. Then two tiny grey furred paws gently grabbed Walter's finger. Angel reassured him, "Don't be sad, Walter. You are here to find that little boy and love him into life again. We will help you. Do you understand?" She asked.

Walter tried to smile, but new tears traced the paths down his cheeks made by countless others today. "I'm just so overwhelmed by all of this. I had no idea it would hurt so much to see what has happened to me over the years." Walter answered.

"Your pain is a perception, Walter, just as your beliefs about reality were when you were ten. Children are so vulnerable to suggestion. Trustingly, they will believe whatever you tell them and never question it. The sad part is, they're not old enough to question their beliefs. They do what they're told for fear of losing the love they have in their lives, even if that love is manipulative." Angel explained.

Walter looked at Angel and then asked if he could pet her. She told him it would be most appreciated. He ran two of his fingers down the back of her soft head and thanked her for being with him.

"Play, Walter, is a matter of doing what it is you love to do, no matter what your age. It's giving yourself permission to do what brings you joy. It's trusting that it's okay to be you, doing what you love the way you want to. It's believing in the integrity of your feelings and by not making anyone else responsible for your happiness. When you stop playing in your life, you become a prisoner of others' opinions, fears, and their perceptions. The creative joy of the moment is lost and your child within begins to die." Angel told him.

"How does someone who has lived for so long within the control of their mind and fears learn to live again?"

asked Walter, still puzzled by so much information.

"You must make all of the parts of your life like play. You must give yourself the freedom to rediscover who you are. More importantly, you have to reestablish a relationship with your soul." she said.

Walter blankly stared at Angel in his confusion. "You don't mean that I have to go to church again, do you?" he quietly asked.

"No, Walter, that's not what I'm saying at all," Angel countered, "but doesn't your meeting with me, under these circumstances, suggest to you that life is far more magical and mysterious than you originally thought?"

"Well, I do have to admit, this is easily the strangest experience that I have ever been through!" Walter exclaimed, recognizing an obvious truth.

"What I mean by your soul relationship, Walter, is for you to touch your personal feelings and your heart and give yourself permission to become who you believe yourself to be. There are no gods, except your own beliefs, Walter. You have become who you are by choice and your belief system. No one, in truth, has ever forced you." She explained.

"You, Walter, have become what and who you are by choosing to believe in others, rather than in yourself. You have made their lives more important than your own." Angel continued.

"You know, you're right, Angel. I haven't thought about what makes me happy for nearly fifty years. I feel like an impersonator who has always tried to be someone else. I'm so tired, and there's been no joy for me at all during the last couple of years, at least until today," Walter confessed. "My biggest fear is whether

I'll have the courage to do what you are telling me I should do. You have to know, I will lose almost all I have, if I follow my heart. I have some serious doubts about all of this that will make it hard for me to let go." he said.

"We understand that, Walter, and for that reason, we have prepared something for you to help you decide. I must tell you, what we are about to show you will not all be pleasant, but it will be done out of love and for your higher good." she explained. "You can back out now, and we will send you back to your body and your world, but you must know, if we do that, nothing will change in you during this lifetime." She warned.

"Can you please tell me what you are going to do?" He asked.

"No Walter, you have to trust in me and in the experiences you will have. They are all designed for your higher good." She answered.

Chapter II: Tom

Angel told Walter to close his eyes. She then asked him to think about the boys that were with him that day in the park playing in the fountain.   She told him, in particular, to think about Tom.

It had been nearly forty years since Walter had seen Tom. The last he had heard, Tom was a successful

plastic surgeon practicing in Hollywood. Walter felt a strange lightness come into his body as he gave himself fully to remembering the boyhood friends of his youth. It was like falling backwards, but he was not afraid, for he felt a presence behind him, supporting him.

The next thing Walter heard was Angel telling him to open his eyes. Before him, stood a large beautiful colonial with a swimming pool and a tennis court. There was a black Rolls Royce and a metallic blue Mercedes Benz parked in the driveway.

"Wow!" Walter exclaimed, "Nice!"

"This is the house of your friend, Tom." Angel told him.

"He must be rolling in the dough! I always knew Tom would be rich some day. He would do anything to make money." Walter told Angel.

"Your perceptions are correct, Walter, and put the emphasis on *anything*." Said Angel.

Walter did not immediately catch the meaning of her jest.

"Your friend, Tom, is under investigation by a government agency for his possible connection to drug trafficking. His greed led him to get involved with the wrong sort of people." Angel told him.

"Will he get off?" asked Walter, who could hardly believe what he was hearing.

"You will have to see that for yourself, Walter. We are going to observe him and his family for awhile. You will not be able to talk to him, but you can watch his life, and his choices unfold." Angel told him. Then Angel climbed up on Walter's shoulder and told him to think himself into Tom's house. She told him he could use his imagination and feelings to do this. Walter closed his eyes and did as Angel instructed. Slowly, he could feel his body moving and then it stopped.

When he opened his eyes again, they were standing in the wide foyer of the magnificent colonial. It must have been fifty yards to the back of the house, thought Walter. The ceiling was at least forty feet high and there was a huge crystal chandelier that hung down from the ceiling high above the foyer. He had never seen such a plush house before. Every forty feet there was a room to go into and each was decorated in a different style. There was even an indoor lap pool with a bar that was as big as any bar he had seen in town.

They followed the white noise sound of a television to a sitting room in the back of the house. Sitting on the couch was a young man about seventeen years old, looking blankly into the blank screen of a TV that had apparently gone off the air. Walter looked at Angel and told her he felt a deep and heavy despair in the room. Angel told him that it was coming from the boy.

"Tom told his family today that he is being charged with drug trafficking and the IRS has taken over his business. Tom will, of course, lose everything." She told Walter. "The young man realizes that with the loss of his father's business income and social status, he will most probably lose his friends, his girlfriend, and his car. It's a heavy burden to carry for someone so young who was used to so much." Angel stated.

"This is horrible! Can't something be done to stop what's happening?" Walter asked in desperation.

"You are seeing the result of a life that was built on outer perceptions and not from the integrity of the heart. Tom equated love with being given things as a child and over his lifetime, it has turned to greed." explained Angel.

"Tom buys everything he has in his life, including his family, his friends, and even his business associates. He doesn't know how to love or appreciate anyone, because he never learned to love and appreciate the good in himself."

"He could have become a gifted psychic healer in this lifetime, doing such good, but he chose to follow the money, instead of his heart. Little did he realize that eventually he would have been just as wealthy, but with peace of mind, as well."

"When he was only sixteen years old, he was visited by his spiritual guide and told of the special gift he had. He decided to be a doctor and he compromised with his heart. The degree could not teach him everything his guide wanted to teach him, but the intense pull of money was too strong for him," Angel explained.

"Don't misunderstand me, Walter. There is nothing wrong with money. But, when you gain it in ways that dishonor your heart or soul's purpose, it then becomes the only purpose in your life, and that can be very dangerous." she concluded.

They walked up an elegant curved staircase to an open balcony, which overlooked the massive foyer and hallway below. In front of them were several upstairs rooms and another hallway that must have been at least a thousand feet long.

After walking about thirty feet, they became aware of someone talking. Walter asked Angel if they could go into the room and she said they could. Sitting on the floor by the bed was a beautiful young girl. She was in tears and talking with someone angrily on the phone. Shocked, Walter heard her say she hated her father and that she was going to run away.

Angel filled Walter in, "Tom never made time to become a friend to his daughter. Business always came first, and the money was used to placate her. Now, during a time when most people need the love and support from their loved ones, Tom is being abandoned. Tom is seeing, firsthand, the Karma, the very result of abandoning his heart. Because he ignored his soul in this lifetime, the false world he created is about to abandon him." Angel explained. "His daughter will be okay, but she'll decide to live her life with a far different set of values, and all because of this experience."

"I never realized how the choices we make clearly create the results that they do. All of this has come about because Tom didn't choose the path of his heart." Walter said, to no one but himself.

Hearing Walter, Angel said, "He would have had all of this anyway, Walter, but his purpose would have been far different. Instead of working just to amass a fortune for money's sake, he would have been working along his heart's true paths that of helping people heal their lives."

They decided that they had seen enough in that room. Walter wanted to do something to help, but Angel told him they could not interfere, for it was not the way of the universe to force itself onto someone. Tom would have to ask the universe for help. Sadly, at this point, Tom and his family were still too concerned about their social faces to see the real need for help.

As they walked further, Walter could see a human figure sitting at a dimly lit desk in what looked to be a den at the end of the long hallway. Angel interrupted his thoughts by saying that this room would have to wait. This would be their last stop. Before going into that room, she first wanted to take him into the master bedroom.

On the king-sized bed lay a very attractive woman who had apparently drunk herself to sleep. Angel explained it to Walter. "She could not bear the reality of losing her possessions. She was taught from early childhood that she would get far with her beauty, if she valued wealth and the men who could build it. It was in this fashion that she caught Tom, because they were both motivated by the exact same things.

They've been married for twenty years now, Walter. They've shared wealth and two children, and yet they have never shared even one honest and innocent emotion between them in those twenty years. What a waste of life." Angel stated.

There was a cold and empty feeling that came over Walter, suddenly, as they left the master bedroom and started down the hall towards the den. Walter mentioned this to Angel, but she said nothing. Sitting there in front of a large cherry roll top desk was Tom.

Upon seeing him, Walter was ecstatic! He was so glad to see Tom that he started to walk over to greet him. Then Angel again reminded him that Tom could neither see nor hear him.

Tom was visibly drunk and taking some pills from a bottle that was in a drawer to his left. On the desktop was a small stack of legal-sized papers, which appeared to be some sort of documents. Walter leaned in and read that it was a subpoena to appear in court.

The sudden sadness Walter felt was overpowering. He never realized that his friend -- the boy he had known from his childhood -- would ever come to this. Innocence dies so young, he thought. "Why did this have to happen, Angel?" he asked in a sorrowful voice.

"Walter," Angel explained, "It's because your friend chose not to follow the call of his heart. Innocence never dies in a heart that stays true to itself, like the heart of a child. Tom chose to take the money and run, so to speak. In the matter of his heart, he sold out. He bet on the dreams of others and in the hollow traditions of your society, rather than listening to his heart, which held the only key to his happiness."

"Your heart, Walter, is not merely a physical organ. It is the epicenter of all feeling and awareness. Life is pure feeling. Life is not just a commodity to be analyzed and tucked away into a pocket to lie forgotten. Your heart connects you to all life on all planes, at all times, and in all places! That is how you are able to see the past of your life now, and how you've come to this place, a thousand miles from the park where we met." she told him excitedly.

Walter watched Tom as he stumbled through a phone book searching for a number. Next, Tom knocked over the drink on the desk beside him, spilling its contents, and he cursed himself. Then as Walter watched, Tom dialed the number he had found in the phone book. Tom let the phone ring for quite some time, before replacing the headset slowly into the cradle again. Tom gave an audible sigh of despair.

In a million years, Walter could not have foreseen what was about to happen. To Walter's horror, Tom suddenly pulled a gun from his lap and shot himself in

the head! Walter was devastated, yet through his tears, he could see Tom's soul leaving his body at the moment of the shot. It was met by two lighted beings that were suitable to his energy at that time.

 Walter was stunned. He thought about Tom, his family, his very life. What a waste! He looked over at Angel, but he was unable to even speak. He had not counted on such a graphic lesson! Finally, sensing

Walter's total dismay, Angel told him to look on the desk at the telephone book where Tom found the number he dialed. His lifeless hand was resting on a worn page with the name of Walter S. Bohring circled in red ink.

"Walter, every time a person dies and their life has been wasted, we sense in some way a sorrowful pity that their potential was not reached. It is especially difficult for those of us here. We know the everlasting beauty of your souls and the immortality of life." she said.

"He was calling to say goodbye to you, Walter, but none of this is your fault. He was still looking outside of himself for what he wanted and needed so badly to find from within -- the love, acceptance, and the very innocence of his youth.

It is not your responsibility to save people, Walter. That is not the purpose of life. Your responsibility lies in saving yourself from your fears, your doubts, and your anxieties by opening up your heart and loving yourself. Each person is given this choice, and a choice is all that it is. No God or devil keeps you in chains. They are merely beliefs and ideas about life. Your heart and its openness is what creates heaven or hell on earth. Your heart will never lie to you. Your heart will never fail you. Your heart will always be true."

Walter looked at Angel, marveling at her keen insight and vast intelligence. Then he asked her, "How does one open their heart? It seems like such an abstract thing. My mind agrees with you, but doesn't fully understand what you're saying. I feel like a baby bird that has not yet learned how to fly."

"That is because the language of the heart is *feelings*, dear Walter. I am not talking about emotions. Emotions are not the same as feelings. Emotions are the result of thoughts which are intensely sent to the subconscious mind and then picked up by the soul. More often than not, they are negative thoughts. These negative thoughts tend to throw you off center. *Feelings* are what you are, Walter. Thinking is a byproduct of conscious awareness. It is like a scout who explores new territory and sends back the information to the military patrol. Your thinking was meant to serve your feeling nature, but fear and doubt about survival have caused your race to ignore the heart and its very nature. To feel, Walter, and to open your heart, you must first dare to become your true *self* and then live your dream.

You must want to do and become that which you love, like a romance with your female species, only the object of your desire is a deeper awareness of your inner self."

Angel motioned to Walter that it was time for them to go. She asked him again to close his eyes but this time, she asked him to remember his friend, Bill. Walter was hesitant to do this, based on what he had seen at Tom's, but Angel said it was necessary and that he would be okay. Slowly, Walter found himself drifting and floating and it was peaceful, healing almost. Then he felt human energy and heard the sounds of a busy neighborhood.

Chapter III: Bill

Angel told Walter to steady himself before he opened his eyes. She wanted to make sure that he felt totally present within his being again. Walter took several deep breaths and slowly opened his eyes.

They were standing in the middle of a street somewhere out in the suburbs. Both sides of the street were lined with houses as far as the eye could see. Walter thought it must be a new development because the trees and bushes around the homes were very small, giving the place a naked and exposed look. Walter felt the area lacked any individual personality. He told Angel it looked like a preppie concentration camp.

"We're going into that house over there, Walter." Angel said, pointing to a beige two-story house about midway down the block on the right side of the street.

"Please tell me nothing bad is going to happen. I don't want to see any more of my friends get hurt." Walter told her sadly.

"This visit will be to see your childhood friend, Bill, Walter. His situation is not as critical as Tom's was, so you can feel at ease." Angel told him.

They walked down to the two-story house and into Bill's home. Walter was shocked. It was a mess! There were dirty plates, ash trays and beer cans all over the living room. The furniture looked new, but there were several gaping tears visible in the upholstery and ugly gouges in the exposed wood of both the chairs and the sofa. Crumpled newspapers were strewn on all the table tops, as were piles of bills and junk mail. He could see even more clutter everywhere else, all throughout the home.

Suddenly the screen door flew open and two children came running into the house. The small boy and girl were filthy, looking as though they had not had baths in nearly a month. They were screaming "Mommy, Mommy, Mommy," as they ran through the rooms and into the kitchen.

"Shut up, you Goddamn brats! Can't you see your

father and I are busy?" Came an angry voice.

Walter thought, "Nice lady" to himself as he and Angel walked into the kitchen just behind the children. There sat Bill -- all 300 lbs of him -- at the kitchen table. Beside him sat a scowling woman who looked like his twin, size-wise, with a cigarette dangling from one side of her mouth. Walter could not believe it. Bill had been such an athletic young man, a fitness freak, even planning to be a coach after he graduated from college, from what Walter remembered. He wondered how the present situation had ever come about.

"Angel began to talk. "Your friend fell in love and he sold out his dreams, Walter. It happens all the time in your dimension, you know. People mistake love for security and get into co-dependent relationships. He had this deep fear of losing control in love and, because he feared it so deeply, he actually caused it. His wife was once young and beautiful, but she, too, had the same fear.

Neither of them has known what they were doing for years. Their main goal in life is to keep up with the Jones's, but that goal has gotten them nowhere but into financial trouble. They're going to have to file for bankruptcy. His job could be enough, but he gives the money to his wife and tells her to buy whatever the neighbors buy. The problem is that in most of those families, both adults work. She isn't able to because of a disability.

"What lousy luck." Walter whispered.

"It was not bad luck, Walter. It was rather a case of making bad choices. Their emotional insecurity caused them to try and rescue each other in the name of love. Now, the straw that broke the proverbial camel's back is here. They don't respect each other and they blame each other for their problems. She will divorce him once the bankruptcy is filed. That's probably good though, because it will provide each of them with a chance to love themselves again. Maybe then they can live out their heart's dream," Angel told him.

"Why is it so hard to make relationships work, Angel?" Walter asked, puzzled.

"Because most people hand over their personal responsibility and control to a fantasy called *love*, instead of finding the true love within themselves. They look for it in another person, instead of believing that love is really there within their own being.

"Bill will be ok, Walter. He will grieve for a time, but he will again remember the fun he had when he was coaching kids. He has the gift of motivational inspiration and, when he begins to love himself again, he will become aware of it once more. It's a love and respect of self, Walter. This is what brings your true gifts to the surface in your awareness. Do not forget that, my friend," Angel told him.

"I won't forget, Angel." Walter answered. "I'm so tired of my life not working out, and I'm weary of wallowing in self-pity all the time, because of it."

Angel told Walter that it was time to leave. Walter asked her whether they were finished, or if there were still others left to observe.

"You have yet to see what Ed and Sid have done with their lives." Angel said.

"Tell me something, Angel," Walter asked. "Why am I being taken to see each of my childhood friends? And why the four that I spent my tenth birthday with?"

"Because they were the best and truest friends you had and at a time when your heart was still innocent and still open. It began to slowly close after that time. Little by little, your mind opened and your heart closed down. It happens that way with most youth. No one tells them it's okay to stay a child at heart. They're programmed to believe that life has its responsibilities and, if they do not do and be like others, then they won't ever have a happy life. Your schools teach your children to think, but they fail to teach them how to *feel*," Angel said, deep in thought.

Then Angel said, "The main reason your world is losing its young people is because they are tired of being mass-produced like hamburgers. These children on your plane are very aware of their individuality, but they find it difficult to open their hearts. Children need adult friends. They need to be respected and listened to. They need to be encouraged and taught how to open their hearts. They need positive, compassionate role models, and unless adults with open hearts show children a better way to live, then your world is destined for an even higher crime rate and even more drug use."

Chapter IV: Ed

Angel told Walter that it was time to go. She again asked him to close his eyes and this time he was to think of Ed and what he remembered about him. Walter again began to feel he was floating as he breathed deeply and, as he did this, he tried to remember Ed. It had been five years since they had last met. It had been at a class reunion.

Ed had always been the proverbial ladies man, thought Walter. Unlike most of the other boys his age,

Ed had girlfriends, even back as far as kindergarten. He was always the handsome one of their small group -- and the one with the best build, too. Walter also remembered Ed was the best dressed man at the reunion.

Suddenly, Walter felt an abrupt stop, almost like a landing. He was hesitant to open his eyes until Angel told him it was all right to. When he did, he saw right away that they were in a very expensive apartment building, complete with a concierge who welcomed everyone into a large lobby.

He watched as the elevator doors miraculously opened on the 20th floor. Ed's apartment was full of all kinds of modern conveniences. Through a vast wall of windows, you had a panoramic view of a modern city. A large screened TV and stereo system filled one main living room wall. A sunken floor held a circular couch, and the floor was carpeted with white plush carpeting. It was truly a sensual and ultra-comfortable high-end apartment.

Walter thought to himself that Ed had done well for himself. Maybe he knew something that Walter didn't -- maybe Ed could even teach him!

"Yes, Walter, you will learn a lot from Ed, tonight." said Angel, reading Walter's thoughts.

Just then, two people entered the room from the main door to the hallway. It was Ed and a drop-dead gorgeous brunette. Ed was really decked out. He took the woman's coat to hang up in a closet, while she stepped down into the sunken living room and gasped at the sight of so much splendor.

Ed told her that she hadn't seen anything, yet. "You should see the bedroom ..." he said with sex oozing in his voice. She acted as though she hadn't heard him.

Ed poured a couple of drinks and headed towards the couch, where she had planted herself. He handed her a drink and she placed it on the coffee table. "You must make lots of money, Eddy." The brunette murmured with a sensual smile.

"Yeah, I'm rolling in dough." He said in his best bravado voice.

"Eddy, tell me about what you do and all about your life." She pleaded.

"Well, as I said earlier at the bar, I'm the president of my own electronics firm. We sell specialty hi-tech computer chips worldwide. It's made me very wealthy," bragged Ed.

Ed sidled a little closer to her on the couch, putting his arm around her. "I've got everything I want, except you, baby." He said suggestively, pulling her closer to him.

She pushed him back, smiling in a teasing manner. "You probably have plenty of women in your life." She said, with a provocative pucker.

"I do, honey, but most of them are bimbo's and they don't interest me like you do. Here, baby, take a drink. its excellent champagne, and very expensive." He said, lifting her drink from the table.

She pushed his hand and the drink away and slid down the couch even further from him. He sighed in frustration and then poured himself another glass of bubbly.

"What about me interests you, Eddy?" she asked, pouting.

"Well, kid, you dress nice and you have a great figure." He told her. "You really make me feel like a man." Ed slid down the couch towards her again. "Now, let's cut the gabbing and get down to business."

"What do you mean?" she asked.

"You know damn well what I mean, shugga. The bedroom is over there." He said, pointing in the direction of the hallway. By this time, he had chugged a fourth straight glass of champagne and his speech was beginning to slur. He had been drinking most of the night.

"I'm not ready for that yet, Eddy. Look, you hardly know me and I need to get to know you better." She said with a confidence she really didn't feel.

Ed angrily grabbed her by the wrist and threw his drink out on the balcony through the open sliders. "Come here, you bitch. You know you want it!" He shouted.

She screamed, and yelled for him to stop. He jumped on her and was trying to undress her. She scratched at his eyes with her fingernails, and he rolled off the couch onto the floor in pain, complaining about his eyes. She jumped up and ran for the door, opened it, and ran screaming down the long hallway.

Ed crawled drunkenly across the floor to the mirror on the other side of the room. He pulled himself up to a sitting position and looked in the mirror. He checked both eyes to see whether either cornea was scratched. Then he began to laugh hysterically and roll on the floor in tears.

Walter was speechless! He stared at Ed in pity and thought to himself how cruel and brutal he had become.

"Your friend, Ed, has never learned the proper value of women. To him, they are objects to be used for sexual gratification and to overcome the boredom in his life. The value he puts on all human life is measured in the external show and never from his heart. He's a very lonely man, Walter." Angel explained.

 "Why do some men have such a hard time with their sexuality and intimacy with women?" Walter asked.

"Angel took a deep breath and continued.   "It's because they lack respect for themselves, Walter. They're ignorant and incapable of even trying to understand the feelings of women.

There is nothing wrong with sex. It's a natural and spiritual gift, but the right time and attitude are everything. Creative energy, or life force, should not be wasted in mindless lust. It should always be in an atmosphere of the deepest sincerity, compassion and with a genuine sensitivity. Two people should not make love together, if they are ignorant of who they are as individuals and without understanding why they are even together. You can only be as close to another human being as you are to knowing yourself."

Angel noticed that Walter looked puzzled.   "What I am trying to say, Walter, is that the mystery of love and sex unfolds when two people know self-love first.   It is not meant to be an emotional prison, but a platform to greater awareness. Neither Ed nor the young woman will ever experience love from another person, until they learn to love and value self first from an open and vulnerable heart."

Walter looked sad. Angel told him to stop punishing himself. "All men are guilty of this behavior, Walter. You and Ed are not the first, and you certainly won't be the last males to be selfish bastards." laughed

Angel.

"Do you know something else, Walter? Animals know better than to rape their own kind. That's because we are creatures of heart and we are in touch with universal love. That's why you think we are so cute. Our very existence is like play for us." She said.

"I'm sorry, Angel. It's just that all of this makes me feel like there is so much to change within us. I could go to a psychotherapist every day for the rest of my life and still not deal with all of my problems." Walter complained.

"Why not go to your heart, Walter. You'll save a lot of time and money." Joked Angel.

"I'm still having trouble understanding what you mean when you say 'my heart'.   I still think of the physical organ inside my chest when you talk about my heart."

"That's okay, Walter. Before we're finished, you'll understand what I mean, she answered.

Angel then told Walter it was time for one last stop. This time they were going to see Sid. Sid was Walter's only black friend. He had a very rough childhood, but Walter always admired his honesty and his keen insight. The last Walter knew, Sid was in the Army and he was due to have been discharged about a year ago.

CHAPTER V: Sid

One last time, Angel told Walter to close his eyes.   She told him to bring his memory of Sid to the front of his mind. Walter chose to think about a high school dance that he and Sid had gone to. Slowly, he again began to float in his thoughts. (This was so peaceful and I'll miss it, he thought to himself). Then he began to pick up some uncomfortable feelings, feelings of desperation, anger and mistrust. He wanted to open his eyes, but Angel had cautioned him against it until he felt more grounded.

When Walter felt his stability return, he opened his eyes. He couldn't believe what he saw. They were under a bridge standing in the center of a group of homeless people. They were dirty and most of them had long greasy hair. There were cardboard boxes set up here and there with people sleeping in them. The whole energy of the place felt sad and understandably oppressive.

Angel told Walter to walk along the left wall of the bridge support and to look where she was pointing. There in a box, all cuddled up like a cat, was Sid.

Walter stooped down to see if he was breathing. Angel assured him that Sid was okay, just sleeping off a drinking spree.

"My God, what happened to him, Angel? The last time I saw him, he was in fine shape," Walter said with dismay.

"He tried to make it in civilian life, but he was not used to ordering himself around. The military had taken care of him for so long, that now he doesn't believe in himself any more, Walter. He was hoping that by getting out of the military, it might give him a better chance to make some money and live a fuller life. He didn't understand that it would take more than military experience to make it." she said.

"But how can people end up like this?" He asked in desperation. "Why are there so many homeless people in America?" Walter was even more confused now.

"For some, it's a conscious choice. Many have given up on your society. They see a lack of depth in your religious, political and business ethics. They are tired of all the lies and the phoniness. In reality, they use these things as excuses to ignore taking personal responsibility for their lives. They believe in nothing. Their hearts are numb and the courage to make a stand is not within them." She stated firmly.

"One of the greatest killers on your planet is heart disease. Do you realize that it stems from a lack of awareness of the true purpose of your heart? Tell me, Walter, do you consider your thoughts and brain to be functionally related?" asked Angel.

"Well, yes," he responded, "I think everyone knows that."

"Where do you think feelings come from?" Angel asked him.

 "Well I guess I'm supposed to say they come from the heart." he replied, uncertainly.

"That's right, but you know the heart doesn't get the same due respect the brain does. The reason is because it's easier for your race to think, than to feel. Most people don't know how to feel. It's a great pity, actually. Your heart and its feelings are the natural pathway to the very healing of your dimension! Every answer you need, as an individual and a race, can come from opening your heart. You are all so caught up with *thinking* that you don't *feel* the marvelous beings that you are!   It's so simple, really, but thinking only makes it seem hard."

Walter looked frustrated again and Angel told him to relax. "Before we're done, you will understand the magic of your heart. Don't worry, Walter, we do not believe in wasting time or energy. This meeting between you and me is not without purpose. Your soul had to create a situation innocent enough to get your attention, and yet painful enough to open your heart.

Each of your friends mirror a thought you hold about existence. You have felt what they have created. You have wondered if their way was correct or was it the easy way out. The truth, Walter, if you will admit to it, is that you are afraid to live and afraid to die. You don't trust yourself."

Tears began to roll down Walter's cheeks, openly. Angel was right. He was basically waiting to die because he didn't know how to live a better life.

"Don't cry, Walter," Angel said, "We are going to show you how to live a better life, if you want to. We cannot make you, but we are willing to show you how." she added.

"Angel, I feel so miserable. I'm so tired of never having any fun or even having the freedom to just enjoy life. I WANT TO LIVE!" Walter shouted.

"Walter, do you feel that crushing pain in your chest?" she asked him.

"Yes, Angel, it feels as though my heart is breaking." he said.

"Not breaking, Walter. It's opening." She replied, with a knowing smile. "Your heart hungers for love and affection. You've ignored it for too long." she told him.

"How can I know love in my heart, Angel? Please, tell me." he begged, openly sobbing.

"I will do more than tell you, Walter. I will show you." She said. "Close your eyes now and think of the tree you were resting under when we first talked." She requested.

Walter wiped at his wet eyes and sat down. Then he closed them. A slight smile played across his face as he remembered how silly he had thought it to imagine that a squirrel could talk. Slowly, Walter began to drift and float into the vast ocean of consciousness that Angel and he had shared. He was grateful for his experiences with her, and hopeful of the way in which she might show him how to open his heart.

Suddenly and unexpectedly, a familiar face flew past Walter. He normally didn't see faces on these little time trips, but this face got his attention.

"It's okay, Walter, don't be afraid." Angel told him in a calming voice.

But it was difficult for Walter. The face he saw was that of his father, and his father had been dead for twenty years. In fact, they had had such a bad relationship that Walter did not even bother going to the hospital the night his father passed away.

There was a nervous sadness on his father's face as he blankly stared at Walter. "Hello, son. It's been a long time." Walter's father told him.

"Hello, Dad, I'm surprised to see you again." Walter answered.

"I know. I also know this is uncomfortable for you, but my guides told me you were ready and that you needed my help." he said.

"Dad, I don't need your help. You never bothered to help me while you were alive, so why would you try now? All you ever did was criticize me, and all of my dreams!" Cried Walter.

"I know, son. I was afraid. I thought I knew all about life. It wasn't until I crossed over, that I remembered the truth. I loved you, Walter, but I realize now how badly I failed you." his father told him.

"You did more than fail me, dad, you ignored me! After you and mom divorced, you went on your merry way." Walter told him sadly.

"I know, son, but it had to be that way. I had to live my life and your mother had yet to find hers. You also needed to become more emotionally secure within yourself, and more reliant upon your own inner life." his father said. "That crisis caused you to question the meaning of your life, to ask about God and why things happen the way they do. Little did you know, it would bring you to this journey." his father said, smiling.

"Hello, Walter!" said a vaguely familiar voice. The face was slowly becoming clearer in the wispy light they all were surrounded by.

"Mom!" exclaimed Walter.

"We don't have much time, Walter, but your father and I wanted to be here. We tried so hard to do what we felt was best for you. I didn't realize until I passed on that I had deprived you of so much of your childhood. I was afraid when your father left, and so uncertain of myself." she told him lovingly.

"You're not angry at Dad?" Walter asked, disbelieving.

"No son, but I wasted much of my life blaming him for the misery I created for myself. We don't want you to do that to yourself." she said, and then continued, "We've come to ask you to forgive us for not helping you discover yourself. We've seen how we manipulated and ignored you, much of the time." she admitted.

"It's okay, Mom. Until this moment, I never realized how much anger I held towards you and Dad. I always wanted to please you and try and make all the pain go away." he told her truthfully.

"Son, you were not responsible for our marriage not working. You are only responsible for yourself. Give yourself the freedom to be all that you want to be and believe you are." his father shared. "We are both truly sorry and ask your forgiveness, Walter."

"I don't know what to say to both of you. Suddenly, I realize that all of my adult life I have been trying to please you. Even though you're gone from my life, I have still been living your dream." reflected Walter honestly.

"We know, son, and we're here to tell you to live your own dream. Don't close your heart. Don't follow the crowd, like we did. You have no idea what is possible." his mother told him.

"Mom, Dad, I love you. Thank you for coming to see me. Of course, I forgive you! I feel so strange right now, like a tremendous weight has been lifted off of me," Walter told them.

"Live your life, Walter, and follow your heart. It will lead you, now that you have forgiven us." said his father.

Angel, who was on Walter's shoulder, told him it was time to say goodbye for now. Walter was not sad, but rather feeling a new peace and sense of freedom that he had never known before. "I know what I want to do." he said.

The images of his parents were fading into the light, as he felt himself floating again in consciousness. Angel told him to be silent and relax. The park began to materialize before him. Angel jumped off of his left shoulder as a sense of continuity came over Walter.

"How do you feel, Walter?" asked Angel.

"I feel great, Angel. It's like I have permission for the first time in my life to be me." he said excitedly.

"Perfect, Walter. So many people think that happiness comes from pleasing others all the time. The truth is, you must give yourself permission to please yourself and to be happy. You will now have the strength and insight to create your own future. Cherish it and follow it wherever it leads you." Angel told him.

Walter looked with love at the furry little friend who had taught him so much. A nervous silence came over him. He didn't want to say goodbye. Angel smiled. Then she told Walter that it had been her privilege to have helped him. "I must leave now, Walter, and you have a prosperous life to live, so please, close your eyes." she told him.

Walter closed his eyes and this time, he began to feel a downward spiral. Then it seemed that everything began to slow down.

"Doctor! Doctor!" shouted a voice. Walter struggled to gain his clarity. He suddenly realized that he was in a hospital bed, his body hooked up to all kinds of tubes. He took several deep breaths, trying desperately to stabilize himself.

"Well, Walter, it's good to see you conscious again. For awhile there, we were concerned you might not make it back," the doctor told him.

Walter tried to speak, but his throat was dry. He simply smiled and nodded at the doctor. He quickly decided not to talk to anyone about his experience. He would keep it to himself. While he was in the hospital, his thoughts were very clear about what he would do with the rest of his life.

The first thing he wanted to do when he got out of the hospital was return to the park. He wanted to reminisce about his journey and feed the squirrels. The doctors told him he would be released in three days.

Walter felt stronger with every day. Finally the day of his departure came and he called for a cab to pick him up. It was a beautiful day. The sun shined through large puffy clouds. The grass was vivid green. The air was clean and fresh and cool. Walter couldn't remember ever being so glad to be alive.

Slowly the cab turned into the park. He paid the driver for the trip and headed over to the tree where he first met Angel. Along the way, he bought a bag of unsalted nuts from a vendor. With the bag in his hand, he sat down on a bench under the tree to wait. This would be his way of showing his gratitude for the joy and wisdom that Angel had taught him.

Slowly, one by one, they came. There must be two dozen squirrels in the immediate area! Walter laughed and spoke to each one as they took a nut from his hands. He felt so good inside.

Then in a somewhat solemn and reverential way, Walter spoke to the memory of Angel. "Angel, I don't know where you are or if you can hear me, but I want you to know that I called my boss while I was in the hospital and I quit my job. I've decided to bring others to this park to feed squirrels. I know it helps a lonely and lost heart to do that. I'm also going to write a book about this experience and, hopefully, share it with the world. I love you, Angel. Thank you for helping me find my path," he spoke to the memory of Angel.

Tears welled up in Walter's eyes as his heart began to burn with a familiar warmth. He had found himself and he had realized that the unseen world did care

about him and all those who were seeking a way home. Suddenly, he felt the paw of a squirrel grip one of his fingers as he had been gazing mindlessly into the sky.

Looking down, he saw the squirrel had a nut in its paw and it was offering the nut to Walter. Walter was half crying and half laughing as he took the nut. The squirrel then winked at Walter before running off into the park to play. Walter thought to himself, life is so full of magic and surprise. You only have to look at it through an open heart and not try and see with your head.

Leaving the park that day, Walter Bohring had another synchronistic experience, one which gave further affirmation to the lessons he had learned. A traffic sign stood at the entrance to the park warning outsiders that inside the park they must always be careful:

CAUTION -- CHILDREN AT PLAY.

Home: Where the Heart Is

Home: Where the Heart is

This is the story of Zevon, a being from the planet, Mauldron, who was banished for antisocial behavior and sent to a distant and outcast planet called Garbon, in the Phoenix Star System. Zevon was a brilliant young man whose parents hoped would someday develop into a capable space physicist.

On Mauldron, mental analytical ability was prized far above all else and those who were prone to excessive feelings or fantasy of any kind were looked upon as being unproductive and non-beneficial to society.

Zevon never felt as though he belonged. He was emotional and prone to spells of imaginary wandering. Instead of working on his computer and solving the complex equations he was given for homework, Zevon could often be found drawing sketches of a robed old man, a pretty young girl, and a beautiful magical land surrounded by crystal mountains. Zevon couldn't understand why he did this, but these were visions that simply appeared to him, unbidden, and he was fascinated by them.

On Zevon's eighteenth birthday, he was to declare his Gatoo, which was his chosen vocation for life. The

Gatoo was an ancient rite on Mauldron and each person, upon reaching the age of eighteen, was expected to comply. This way, social order was maintained, everyone was a productive citizen, and the family lineage was upheld in Mauldron society.

Zevon was considerably nervous about this coming rite, because he knew deep inside that he could not honor the ancient code of his people. Something was always gnawing at him to honor himself first and to follow his heart. The only problem with this was that on Mauldron, failure to keep the Gatoo ritual meant being banished to Garbon, rumored to be a desolate uninhabitable planet in the Phoenix Star System, at least until you came to your senses.

The Mauldonian leadership had learned over the centuries that fear was a powerful tool. Fear was used to keep the social order intact. If they didn't banish the undesirables, people would begin to think and believe all sorts of senseless ideas and become emotional, all things which were unusual, odd and hard to understand.

On Mauldon, painting, poetry, singing and acting were all considered to be unlawful and punishable by banishment. All who were caught in these activities, as well as in emotional outbursts, were to be taken to court, imprisoned, and sent to far away planets, such as Garbon, to contemplate their sins and repent.

Zevon's parents were middle class Mauldronites with great pride and they held an excellent social standing. His father was a space physicist, his mother, a space shuttle operator. Both were good people, but to Zevon, they seemed cold and unfeeling. They never answered his questions about the feelings he held inside, nor did they explain where the feelings came from. His parents knew that to do so would cause him pain in later life, not to mention, great psychological damage. They chose to ignore his questions.

Mauldron's great philosophers had determined long ago that following one's feelings would lead to a condition known as Ahlgood, a mental illness where the person appeared to be in a heightened state of awareness and happy to the point of bliss. This was deemed wrong and unnatural by Mauldon's standards for high mental acuity.

The problem for the Mauldronites was that this condition threatened their highly productive and analytical society. Physical achievement was prized above all else and anything that didn't follow their definition of physical achievement, as well as mental acuity, was deemed to be highly taboo and punishable by long-established Mauldronian law.

As the ritual of Zevon's Gatoo approached, Zevon found himself agonizing over what he would do. In his heart, he knew he could not commit to any specific Mauldronian vocation. Zevon also knew that it would be useless to try and deceive the Grand Council before whom he would have to appear. He was also concerned about his female friend, Clika.

The computers determined she would be a perfect match as a genetic mate and an excellent mental companion for Zevon. Clika was more than he could ever have dreamed of, yet he sensed something critical was missing from their relationship. She was beautiful and kind and had excellent genetic qualifications, but there was something innately boring about their relationship and he could not understand why.

Zevon agonized over everything inside that made him different than the rest. In his heart, he knew he wasn't wrong. This was who he really was, but he would have to make the most important decision of his life in the next few days. He also realized he could no longer hide behind the innocence of being too young.

Terror gripped his heart as he thought about facing the truth inside, because he feared that all he had known and cared for would be lost, if he stood up for himself and what he wanted and believed in. His parents would be disgraced and Clika would leave him. Still, something silently nagged at him, "Isn't it better to trust in your feelings, than to always be a prisoner to your thoughts?"

Zevon couldn't stop thinking about Garbon, and what he had heard some say about the planet. Supposedly, it was a hell to behold and many who were sent there never returned. Those who did come back seemed glad to be home, but for some reason, they were never quite the same after. There was a beaten look to their faces, which said something about the condition of their soul.

Zevon began to cry as he pondered his fate. For a moment, he thought sadly about taking his life, but as he lay in his bed in the darkness, a voice spoke to him from in his thoughts. "Zevon, you must go to Garbon." He was startled for a moment and asked, "Who's there?" He turned on the light and looked quickly around the small room. The voice had sounded so real! He expected to see someone standing there, but he was alone. Zevon laid back down, and thinking again about Garbon, he fell into a deep and troubled sleep.

Chapter I: THE RITUAL OF GATOO

The ritual of Gatoo was a grand spectacle on Mauldron. It was always held in a special laboratory amphitheater which seated all of the members of the Grand Council, several technicians, and there was still room enough for the initiate's family and their friends, as well.

In the middle of the amphitheater, was a chair called The Seat of Ascension, aptly named because once the initiate passed the rite, he immediately assumed a role in Muldronian society. Full privileges went to all who passed their ritual and, for the rest of their life, they would lack no real physical need. Since the normal Mauldronite lived to the ripe old age of 200 years, that would mean a lot of physical pleasure. To Zevon, that didn't matter at all, if he had to ignore what he knew was important to him.

The seat, itself, was hooked up to the main computers of Mauldron. Wires were attached to the initiate to monitorhis responses to questions from the Grand Council. The sole purpose of the computers was to give accurate data as to an initiate's suitability to join the elite Mauldronian society.

The initiate was then grilled for several hours on all laws, responsibilities, and customs of Mauldronian life. In the final phase, they were asked to take an oath and receive a special implant in their brain. The implant was a computer chip that enhanced the mental abilities and regulated emotions to the point of moderating all emotional outbursts.

The Mauldron Counsel had perfected a technique to gain access to all pertinent information about anyone's life from these chips. There was no need to consider feelings of the heart, because a thought directed to the mind would send an electronic signal to the main computer to give an appropriate response. It was a painless procedure, but it was permanent, and the chip was only removable upon the person's death.

Zevon was brought from a side room to the Seat of Ascension where the technicians hooked him up to the electrodes. Zevon could see his friends, family and the Council and he was apprehensive.

When they finished with the wiring, the Grand Counselor, Omien II, began by asking Zevon if he understood the reason for the proceedings and if he knew the great honor it was for him to be here. Zevon told them he knew the reason for the proceedings and thanked the Grand Counselor for the privilege of being there.

For two hours, Zevon was asked all manner of questions about Mauldonian life and his studies in space physics. He answered each question impeccably and without hesitation. His parents beamed with pride as they watched their son handle himself with such confidence and assurance. The time had now come for Zevon to take the oath of allegiance to Mauldon. The Grand Counselor commended Zevon for his handling of the questioning and then began the oath:

"DO YOU, ZEVON OF MAULDON, SWEAR BY ALL OF YOUR ABILITIES AND SKILLS TO FAITHFULLY SERVE THE SOCIETY OFMAULDON AND OBSERVE IT'S HONORED TRADITIONS? "

Zevon tried to say "I do," but his uncertainty made his throat dry and the words came out in a squeak. The counsel requested that he speak louder and more clearly. Again he looked at his friends and family and tried to say "I do," but now he realized that something inside of him was restraining the perfect response that he had planned. Again he heard the voice in his thoughts. "Zevon, you must go to Garbon."

At that moment, one of the monitoring technicians motioned to the Grand Counselor that a reading of deep emotional unrest was appearing on their monitoring system.

The room became very still and the pride on their faces turned to looks of concern. Zevon sat in his chair, embarrassed and angry at himself and fearful of what the next few minutes would bring. As he looked at his family and Clika, he could see the shame on their faces and, for the first time, he realized he was completely alone. No matter how much he tried to act like the rest of them, something inside would not allow it, because he knew -- he was not like the rest.

The Grand Counselor asked Zevon if he knew why the computer was registering such a deep emotional response to the oath. Zevon said that he did not know. The Grand Counselor smiled at Zevon and the others and said they would simply try again. The Counselor read the oath once more and, as it came time for him to respond, this time Zevon looked at the Grand Counselor and the others and, taking a deep breath and holding tight to his unspoken beliefs, he told them that he could not take the oath.

There was a powerful silence in the chamber. The seriousness of the consequences, now more than ever before, were apparent to Zevon. With total resignation, he realized he could not hide the truth any longer. He was now an outcast, but he was prepared to do whatever he had to do. He had to be true to himself.

The Grand Counselor asked Zevon if he understood the seriousness of his situation and what the end result would have to be if he failed to take the oath. Zevon looked the Counselor directly in the eyes and said that he did. Zevon had gone this far and now he was determined to follow his feelings.

The Grand Counselor sat in silence for a moment, incredulous at this young man's attitude and negative response. How could such a talented and promising young man so easily turn his back on family, friends, and his very society?

Slowly, the Grand Counselor stood. With righteous indignation etched on his face, he looked out over the entire Gallery and into each face of those sitting in the great room. Taking a deep breath, he loudly proclaimed with serious finality that Zevon had failed the initiation into Mauldonian Society. He announced that he had no choice but to send him to the planet Garbon to think about and reconsider his choice. Now, as was customary in Mauldonian Society, the entire Gallery stood. In one simultaneous motion, as was their custom, they turned their backs to the outcast initiate.

Zevon understood the consequences. He would not see his family or female friend ever again. Zevon managed to contain his composure as the Counselor made his pronouncement, but as they took him to the holding chamber to wait for extradition to Garbon, he began to sob and think about his fate. Zevon had never felt so alone and rejected. Even the escorts who were in charge of seeing him to the planet Garbon had been cold and indifferent. For the next twenty-four hours, he would be in a minimum security holding room as they waited for the shuttle to Garbon.

As he lay in his bed that night, be bemoaned his fate and all that had brought him to this, but with a strange curiosity, he wondered what he might find on the planet Garbon. He was sad to be leaving the only life he had ever known, but he also felt relieved that he no longer had to hide his innermost feelings. While his mind pondered the many horrible stories about

Garbon, his heart began to dream and with that, he fell into a deep and fitful sleep.

Chapter II: The Trip To Garbon

"Get up!" nudged the shuttle operator, "it's time to go!"

Zevon groggily tried to pull himself together as he was led down a long tunnel and into the waiting space craft. The trip was not going to be a long one, but for where he was going, he wished it were. The idea of being alone on Garbon to review his decision was not a joyful enterprise he looked forward to -- not at all.

The shuttle operator shouted at him to buckle up and Zevon quickly complied. The few shuttles to Garbon were small two-man crafts that were only for short to minimum range flights from Mauldon. It would take six hours to make the trip from which Zevon was not sure he would ever return. The only thing that was on his mind at the present was the voice which spoke to him the night before he was to make his Gatoo. "You must go to Garbon!"

Just then, the shuttle operator broke the silence and asked Zevon if he might share some information with him. Zevon agreed. The operator told him he had taken many people to Garbon. Most were already broken in spirit or gave in, after only a short period. After a short pause, he continued by saying that he had heard of some on Garbon who liked it there and seemed to enjoy the experience, although he didn't know any of the particulars.

Zevon thanked the shuttle operator. He felt relieved. This was the first time that anyone had said anything at all about other inhabitants being on Garbon.

The operator cautioned Zevon that he should be on the lookout, though, for one character named Anggar from the Nebula, Deblon. He stated that he was extremely dangerous and someone to be feared and avoided at all costs.

Zevon had heard of the Deblonites. He heard it said that they were an ancient people who prided themselves in their physical domination over other races. They were also known to practice cannibalism.

The operator told him that Garbon actually had many unusual races of beings on it, but Anggar was to be avoided if Zevon was to survive. Of course, the mere thought of cannibalism repulsed Zevon, so he made up his mind that he would do everything he could to avoid this Anggar being.

It was now four hours into the flight and Zevon was relieved that some of the unknown about this trip was now known. He was anxious to meet the other outcasts, but not happy about having to watch out for the Deblonite, Anggar. He thought to himself that it would be best to think on the positive side and not worry about the negative right now.

Chapter III: Garbon

Zevon kept his eyes focused on the huge octagon-shaped window in the ceiling of the shuttle. Suddenly, a large planet came into view off in the distance. That had to be Garbon, he thought. He had been told that it was a planet nearly the size of Mauldron, but it wasn't at all as civilized or developed. The reality was, Garbon was a galactic junkyard, populated by all sorts of rejected people and objects which had all been judged useless for whatever reason.

The shuttle operator warned Zevon to tighten his seat straps to prepare for a hard landing. He said the landings were usually safe, but due to the atmosphere around Garbon, sometimes turbulence caused a rough landing. Zevon complied, but the warning proved to be unnecessary. The shuttle landed easily and came to a gentle stop.

As the shuttle was closing in on the landing field, Zevon noticed that Garbon certainly lived up to its reputation. The terrain was barren, almost desert-like and, at least on this
area of the planet, there seemed to be very few trees and he could see no water anywhere. The closer they got to the surface, the more the personality of the planet affected Zevon. He sensed a desolate, eerie aura and it gave him the feeling of things left behind and discarded. This made him feel anxious and empty.

The operator startled Zevon out of his reverie. "Well here you are. Watch your step getting out."

Zevon asked, "What do I do next?" But the shuttle operator only pointed toward some trees in the distance and told him he'd better start walking, because the trees were about a day's journey away.

"Everything you will need to survive will be found there."

Zevon thanked him for his candor and advice and, as he stepped down onto the ground and backed away, the shuttle lifted off the planet and quickly sped from sight. It would be three months before another shuttle would stop to evaluate Zevon's situation.

Fearful and without companionship, Zevon began the day's walk to the tree line in the distance. All along the way, in front and all around him, he could see nothing but rusted and wrecked machines, computer pieces, and abandoned or smashed spacecraft parts. Zevon thought, what a dump. Maybe the trees up ahead will provide a better view.

It wasn't even three hours since the space shuttle left the planet and already Zevon was thirsty. He didn't know where to even start to look for water -- he wasn't real sure there was any water on Garbon.

After walking another half hour or so, he came to a small puddle inside the burned out carcass of a spacecraft that had apparently been sheltered from the warm Garbon Sun. As he stooped over to drink, he caught a motion out of the corner of his eye. As he turned his head to the right, his heart began to pound in fear. He had never seen such a frightful looking creature. It stood nearly eight feet tall, was covered with hair, and yet it wore a leather vest.

On closer inspection, he found it interesting that the being's upper half looked animal-like and yet its lower half seemed to be made of some sort of metal. It resembled an odd kind of animal/robot. Strange, very strange, Zevon thought to himself. Slowly he moved back, so he wouldn't be seen. Then as he watched in apprehension, the creature growled and picked up a machine that had to have weighed half a ton and threw it through the air. Zevon gasped and felt his heart literally jump into his mouth. The beast heard and, as it slowly turned in Zevon's direction, it began to sniff the air.

"Who's there?" the beast shouted angrily.

Zevon was so silent that the beating of his heart was the only sound he could hear -- and right now he wished it was even more quiet than that. As Zevon peeked from where he was hiding, he noticed the beast had moved out of sight. He decided it would be wise to use the huge pieces of wreckage as cover. He would slip out into the distance and away from this awful being.

Slowly he moved from wreck to wreck, then crouched down, until he had gone several hundred yards away from the site. Then he stood up and saw that the beast was still there, but in the wreckage and looking around there. Zevon knew he was safe. His heart was slowing to normal again and he noticed the trees were closer than before.

Suddenly, a thought came to Zevon. Anggar! That must have been Anggar that he saw back there! Actually, he was relieved that he had seen his adversary before he accidently stumbled upon him. He knew what Anggar looked like now and where he was, at least for the time being.

The tree-covered area did not relieve much of the anxiety Zevon had about the planet. It covered about one square mile and had some deep parts to it, but he saw this area, too, was filled with wrecks, garbage and underbrush. There were some ramshackle huts that had apparently been built by others to protect themselves from exposure, but they certainly weren't first class accommodations. In the part of

the forest where he had entered, there was a small pond that looked to be clean and clear. He tasted the cool water and it seemed to be okay.

A few hundred yards further, he found a shack where he would sleep for the night. On closer inspection, a few of the trees contained some sort of fruit that would provide nourishment -- at least for the time being. Feeling tired, Zevon entered the shack.

Once inside, he was shocked to finally come face-to-face with the awful place he had been banished to. A skeleton lay in the corner, it's bleached bones resting against the dilapidated wall. With that, Zevon decided to rest outside under a tree that was surrounded by bushes for cover. Undecided about what to do next, but physically and emotionally exhausted, Zevon fell into a deep sleep.

Chapter IV: The Dream

Where am I? Thought Zevon, as he stared into a light in front of him. He felt muddled and unsure. It was as if he were dead or maybe hallucinating. He wasn't afraid, actually. For some reason, the light held him unmoving. and it's warmth gave him no reason to want to leave.

Suddenly, a face appeared within the light and it smiled at him. "Hello, Zevon!" said the being.

Smiling back, Zevon said, "Hello, who are you?"

The being told Zevon he was called the Greeter at the Gate. Zevon thought, what gate? The only thing he could see was a smiling face in the light and a deep pervasive fog that seemed to be everywhere.

Zevon hesitantly asked if he were dead. The Greeter laughed and told him he wasn't dead -- he was only but we didn't think you would believe that, so we've arranged this meeting with you."

"What are you talking about? What meeting?" Zevon asked the Greeter.

"We have so little time. I must ask you to listen very

carefully, Zevon."

Surprised by the Greeter's urgency, Zevon said he would listen to what the apparition had to say.

"You've come to this planet to discover your heart's desire and to fulfill your higher purpose. This was no accident, Zevon. It was preordained. There are others here that you will meet and, like you, they've also traveled a long way on a very similar path of discovery. Do you understand?"

Zevon was puzzled by this stranger and the dream. If there were others here on Garbon who were like him, he wondered where they were. Why hadn't they shown themselves? The Greeter seemed to hear his thoughts. He told Zevon that when it was time, he would meet them, but he must not give in to fear.

"Trust in yourself, Zevon, and trust in the reasons for your being here. You are about to discover a wonderful truth and a joy that is beyond your mind's comprehension."

Zevon began to cry, but he wasn't in pain. Slowly the tears ran down his face, a face that, oddly, he hadn't realized existed in the dream, up to this point. He perceived himself only as a being on the planet of Garbon. He did not feel himself as a body, as such.

As he watched, one tear dropped from his face onto the ground. Then something very strange happened. As he continued to watch, a miraculous thing happened. The tear dissolved right before his eyes into pure light and then transformed into a beautiful rose which then turned into a pure-white dove. The graceful dove flew to his shoulder and then it gently kissed him.

"I must leave now," The Greeter interjected. "It's time for you to go now, Zevon."

Zevon, filled with appreciation for everything he had experienced, thanked the Greeter. He asked when he would see him again. The Greeter smiled and told Zevon, "You can see me every time you sleep and dream." Zevon looked on as the Greeter seemed to dissolve into the light. As he disappeared, he said, "Remember, Zevon, do not give in to the fear."

Chapter V: Anggar and the Princess

Zevon was jolted out of his sleep by a driving punch to the shoulder. He tried desperately to gather his wits together to see what had happened. Focusing his eyes on the being standing in front of him, he realized he was staring into the eyes of the one being he did not want to deal with on this planet. There stood Anggar, his eyes intense, his stance threatening.

Zevon wanted to scream, but who would even hear him? The lump in his throat and the memory that he was not to give in to fear stopped him from coming totally unglued. As a matter of fact, he didn't understand how or why he was able to, but he actually relaxed and did nothing at all.

Suddenly, a feminine voice broke the silence. It seemed to come from somewhere beyond where Zevon sat, semi-paralyzed. "Anggar!" The voice called out. Anggar grunted some sort of unintelligible sound. The voice called out again, "Come, Anggar, let's play. We haven't much time left before we must go back."

The beast seemed tamed by the sound of the female voice coming from beyond Zevon's sight. Zevon smiled. He was thinking to himself that the beautiful voice would tame just about anyone, anywhere at all. Slowly, Anggar ambled away and, just as slowly, Zevon stood up to try and get a glimpse of the person whose voice had commanded such amazing control over the beast. Looking through some bushes, he could only hear some muffled talk, because the beast completely overshadowed the person in front of it.

As luck would have it, right at that moment the beast stooped down and up onto his shoulder climbed the most beautiful girl Zevon had ever seen. She sat on Anggar's shoulder while he galloped around like a horse and she laughed and patted his head. It was an odd sight -- a giant beast that was half machine, half animal, and this tiny wisp of a girl with huge expressive eyes, light brown curls, and wearing the most adorable impish smile he'd ever seen.

Suddenly, Anggar turned towards Zevon's hiding place and pointed right to it. The girl looked puzzled and then became cautious as Anggar began to amble around in circles and grunt his displeasure. She climbed higher, up around his neck, and hid herself in his massive mane.

Zevon wasn't sure what to do. He instinctively felt like running, but on the other hand, this girl was the first human being he had seen on Garbon and he needed help. Forcing himself to relax, Zevon slowly stood up as Anggar approached him. Zevon could see the girl peeking through Anggar's mane and, not knowing what else to do, he nervously said, "Hi".

Anggar immediately growled, and the blast of the roar knocked Zevon backwards and onto his rear end. The girl began to laugh uncontrollably. "Don't be afraid. He won't hurt you." She said. "He's very protective and only making sure you're not planning to harm me."

Zevon picked himself up off the ground and did the only thing he could do that appeared safe. He smiled.

"What is your name?" Asked the girl.

"I'm Zevon."

"That's a nice name." She told him. "Don't you think so, Anggar?" But Anggar growled and glared at Zevon.

"I don't think he likes me at all." Zevon told her warily.

"Oh, he's just being protective, that's all," she defended. "I assure you, he won't do anything to you, unless you appear to be a threat. You won't harm me, will you?" asked the girl.

"No ma'am!" Zevon exclaimed truthfully. "But I thought he could talk." He said, puzzled.

The girl told Zevon that Anggar could talk, but only when he was calm and in control of his reasoning capabilities. When he felt threatened, or felt the need to be protective of her, he regressed to the beast half of his nature.

The girl asked Zevon where he was from and why he was out here. Zevon explained how he was banished to Garbon as punishment for not joining his planet's society. He told her he couldn't do that because, unlike most other Mauldronians, he wanted to do other things with his life. He went on to explain how mechanical his planet was and how they had no room for change nor did they welcome new ideas.

The girl listened to every word he said. Feeling his sadness and frustration, she began to cry softly. Zevon felt a lump in his own throat and unshed tears burned behind his eyelids.

"So you are alone with no one to talk to," the tiny waif stated matter of factly.

Zevon nodded without speaking. Then he told her he would not see anyone from his planet for three months, or maybe even longer. In the meantime, he was forced to do the best he could to survive.

Suddenly out of the blue, Anggar spoke to Zevon. "We will be your friends and help you find your way."

As Zevon looked at the beast, the once fierce eyes were now full of sympathy. Zevon said, "I didn't believe you would care or feel anything about me."

Anggar countered by saying, "You have a good and innocent heart and, like me, you were abandoned by your people because you were different. I feel your pain and I would be proud to be your brother."

With that they all grinned and, in some magical way, their hearts were forever bonded. Zevon then asked the girl what her name was. She told him she was Princess Xela of Harmony. Her planet was several hundred light years away from Garbon and on what she called a different plane of vibrational frequency.

Zevon liked her name very much and told her so. Then as she had done, he asked why she was here. She told him she came to Garbon with her Grandfather to escape the tyranny of their homeland. Her society was also trying to hold onto antiquated traditional views and they disallowed anyone's ability to create their own reality.

"Create your own reality?" Asked Zevon, "What's that?"

Xela told him it was only the greatest gift in the entire universe. It was an ability to choose the reality you want and then live it fully. "You see Zevon, the universe belongs to those who have heart and are not afraid to live by it. For centuries, the people of your galaxy have prided themselves in their knowledge and technology.

What is so unfortunate is that the end result has always been fear, limitation, stagnation, and the veritable oppression of those who were different. Those different ones are always the ones who have heart and feel out of step with the masses. Their challenge is to trust their heart and to learn to live by the power of their inner feelings. You have come here, Zevon, to learn about your heart and to trust its ability to guide you in a further realization of your own personal power."

Zevon admired Xela and he understood what she was saying.

"You see, Zevon, at this moment, my words are being verified by your heart. You know I speak the truth".

For the first time since he'd been on this planet, Zevon had the strongest feeling that his being here was no accident. He also felt sure that the restricted and oppressed feelings he had felt all of his life were about to be removed. Zevon asked Xela what he should do to learn more about his heart and how to trust in it. Xela told him she couldn't help him further, but she felt certain that her Grandfather could help him understand the power of his heart and the laws of creating his own reality.

Zevon was happy to hear that and asked Xela when he could see her grandfather. She told Zevon that her grandfather lived in a deep cave, far below Garbon in a special place and no one could go there without her help. "Zevon, are you sure this is what you really want? The trip is extremely dangerous and life as you know it will forever be changed. You will have to leave all of your excuses behind and learn to believe in the totality of who you are."

Zevon thought about what she said. Then he told her, "All my life, I've had this gnawing sense of being different from others and unacceptable as I am. You and Anggar are the first beings who accept and not judge me. I am afraid, yes, but my heart tells me that this is the direction I must go."

"Wonderful!" cried Xela, "you have the first quality of heart that is required of all those who wish to change. It is the courage to take risks. We will rest for tonight but in the morning, we will start out for the underground cave where my grandfather lives."

Chapter VI: The Journey - Grandfather's Cave

It was morning and, for the first time in who knows how long, Zevon was glad to be alive and looking forward to something. Then as he stood to stretch, he was suddenly sobered to see that he was alone.

Anggar and Xela were both gone. For a moment, fear rose in Zevon's chest. Then, looking around, he spotted a note stuck to a branch of the tree directly in front of him. He was relieved to read that they were sorry to have to leave him, but it was necessary. It was imperative that Zevon learn to develop trust in himself and with this they could be of minimal assistance. The note further explained that he had everything he needed to find the cave. He was to listen to his heart and trust in his feelings.

At first, Zevon felt tremendous frustration and he was saddened to the point of tears. He was alone again. Then something wondrous happened. His chest began to burn warmly and a peace came over him that he didn't fully understand. He also felt a strange change in his awareness for the very first time.

Suddenly he didn't know how he knew, but he knew which way to start out on his journey. Zevon was ecstatic. He couldn't remember ever feeling so good or so secure in his entire life. He had never felt so confident or sure about anything, either. It was like someone else was living inside him and knew just what to do.

After walking for about a mile, he came to what looked like a swamp. His first thought was that this must be a mistake. He must have gone in the wrong direction. But as he listened to his heart and asked for conformation, he felt the assurance he needed. The only problem was, he would have to swim through it and that did not appeal to him. It was anyone's guess as to what might lie waiting just below the surface of the murky, fetid water.

For about an hour, Zevon alternately swam and walked as he made his way through the swamp. Then he saw something moving towards him from the right and he stopped. He couldn't tell what it was, because it was just below the waterline. He could see that it was large because it created waves as it moved. The uneasiness was overpowering as Zevon stood completely motionless. He waited to see what would happen.

Suddenly, the water became calm. Beads of sweat formed on his face, as an eerie chill crept up the back of his neck. He turned slowly to see what was behind him and then he let out a bloodcurdling scream.

In a blinding panic, Zevon both ran and swam to evade the creature. He had never seen such a horrible and evil-looking beast. It resembled a gigantic lizard, covered in scales, with the face of a skeleton. It's claws were eight inches long, and the huge mouth seemed to be snapping at him with razor-sharp fangs. The spikes on top of its head could so easily impale, if he allowed the creature to get that close.

Zevon continued to swim and run until he couldn't muster the strength to move another muscle. He chose then to stop and look behind him. Slowly he turned, hoping he was not still being pursued. He never wanted to see that creature again, although he feared it would haunt his nightmares for a long time.

The creature was gone. Zevon had never felt so relieved, or exhausted, in his life. He was so elated that he began to laugh at himself. He thought his scream must have scared the creature almost as bad as the creature had scared him!

With a lingering smile on his face, Zevon finally exited the swamp and, as he turned to continue on his way, he found himself face-to-face with the creature from the swamp! It had somehow sneaked in front of him as he stood there laughing! Zevon fainted.

Chapter VII: The Detour

"Hello, Zevon," said a familiar voice. "Having a nice time?"

Zevon collected his thoughts, and then answered, "Am I dead?

"No, but then, you are not consciously on Garbon at

this time, either." said the being who was standing in front of Zevon. "You have fainted and left your body, temporarily, to come and see me."

Zevon then asked the strangely dressed being who he was. The being told him his name was Aklar and explained that he was a trans dimensional teacher. Zevon asked him what it was that he taught, and Aklar said he helped people learn to deal with their fears.

"You see, Zevon, many people aspire to follow their hearts and to know their heart's deepest desires, but fear, anger, and doubt all close down the path to their heart. You, too, must learn that you're in charge of all your experiences.

Nothing can harm you, unless you wish it to. Your mind's unconscious memory and programming are what hold you captive to fear. This prevents your heart from revealing the truth. For you to create your own reality, you must trust your heart implicitly and place your mind in subjugation to your heart." Aklar told him.

Zevon told him it was hard to believe his heart when he was facing a creature that made him want to vomit. Just looking at the beast made him sick.

Aklar said appearances are merely perceptions and, besides, maybe Zevon's appearance sickened the creature! "Besides," said Aklar, "that creature is more evolved than even you are. He is a guide. He will assist you in your journey to the cave. He is a very loving being, Zevon, and someone to be trusted. His name is Zook."

Zevon thought about all of this for a minute. He was embarrassed that he had overreacted and freaked out. Boy, had he been wrong! This planet really was a strange place. Laughing, Aklar told him he had more than freaked out. He would have to wash his clothes to remove the feces from them once he returned to his body. Zevon grimaced, "I did *that*, too? Oh no ..."

"One more thing," Aklar said, "you must never apologize for being yourself. No matter what you do, it's perfect for the learning that you need at that time. Remember, you create these situations to discover knowledge about yourself and about your power to choose.

Aklar's words seemed to melt into Zevon's being and become one with him. He felt courage and strength growing inside and, as he looked down, he could see right through his own body. Then he remembered that he was not really here speaking with Aklar. He was actually passed out with feces in his pants and back on the weird planet of Garbon.

Aklar told Zevon it was time for him to return to his body on Garbon and deal with Zook. Zevon looked into Aklar's smiling face and, as Aklar faded into a mist of light, Zevon heard him say, "We love you Zevon. We always have and we always will."

Zevon went back into his body with a thud, partly because of the emotional energy around it and partly because of the fact that Zook would be there. When he became conscious again, he decided to play dead for a while until he could see what had happened.

The first thing he noticed was, he was no longer in the water. He also felt heat coming from a source close to him. The thought that he was going to be roasted alive came to mind. Finally, a voice spoke up and said, "You can stop playing dead now."

Slowly and painfully, Zevon opened his eyes. It was Zook speaking to him. He asked Zook how he knew he wasn't dead or still unconscious. Zook told him that his heart told him.

Zevon asked, "You have a heart?"

"Yes." Zook answered, looking hurt. "All creatures have hearts and souls."

With that, Zevon began to feel better about himself in this situation. He quickly became aware that he was naked and when he looked around for his clothes, he noticed they were drying by the fire.

Zook explained to Zevon that when he took his body from the water, he smelled so bad, he decided to wash and dry the clothes. He also said that there was a thick brown paste all over the inside of them. Zevon could only blush and thank him for all he had done.

The rest of the day was spent discussing the history of the planets, Mauldron and Garbon. Zevon found out that there had been a war before Zevon was born and Mauldron had conquered Garbon. To further punish Garbon, most of its lush and green landscape had been turned into a dump for old space ships, machine parts and computer equipment not needed on Mauldron. The contamination alone nearly killed all the vegetation on Garbon and the few people who survived the war starved to death.

Zook explained that, at one time, his race did eat Zevon's kind, but that changed when they met the old man in the cave. The old man taught them dignity, self-respect, and the true nature of their being. Zook told him that long ago, he was full of hate, pity and anger, but that time was in the past. Anyway, the old man told Zook and the others of his kind that if they truly wanted to heal themselves, they must find some Mauldronians to help on their way. So, for three hundred years, Zook and the others had been helping Mauldronians to find the cave and the old man. "Your people think that most people who came here have perished, but that is not true." Zook told him.

Zevon asked Zook where the people were then, but all Zook would say was, "In good time. All in good time. First you must rest and get your strength back. The journey is a long one and it's very dangerous."

As they sat by the fire that evening, Zevon shared his story with Zook about how strange his life had been. For such a long time, he had felt odd and like an outcast among his own people. He was told many times that his way of thinking was wrong and to put his foolish notions aside. Then when things looked darkest and he was condemned to Garbon, his life finally began to make some sense.

Zook smiled sleepily at Zevon and told him that this was the way it happened when one followed their heart instead of their head. The heart is flexible, infinite, and unlimited, while the head is stubborn, narrow-minded and arrogant. You were simply forced to choose your heart over your head.

Zevon smiled back, feeling such relief. He was finally beginning to understand why he had felt different for so long. Zook then told him it was time to go to sleep.

Chapter VIII: Two of a Kind

It was finally morning. Zevon woke Zook and told him he was ready to begin the journey. Zook yawned and stretched his long reptilian body. Then he said, "Patience, please, Zevon. The trip will take us several days and we are in no hurry. You have to understand that between here and the cave there are many dangers and obstacles."

Zook told Zevon that the terrain and the climate were harsh and that they will have to pace their journey in order to survive. Zevon was impatient, but he had to agree. He didn't have a clue about what lay ahead. He would have to rely on Zook for his guidance. Zook said the cave where they were headed was hidden deep in the jungle, where the mountains rose high into the sky. He further explained that the journey to the old man would take them through the cave, several miles beneath the surface, and down into the planet's very core.

Zevon asked Zook why the cave and the old man were in such an isolated and difficult place to get to. Zook could only tell him that the place where the old man lived was very special and it had a magical effect on all who came there. "Negative energy is not permitted in the cave, Zevon." Zook warned.

"Why is that?" Zevon asked. He couldn't imagine a place that was magical, let alone one where energy -- negative or positive -- could be sensed.

"Zook stated that negative energy would only drain its magical power and the old man would be forced to leave. It's one of the only places left in the entire galaxy where pure love and healing energy can exist." Zook told him almost reverently.

Again Zevon asked how that could be so, and Zook told him, "Because most people on this material plane put greater value in their minds and their thoughts than in their hearts and imagination."

Zevon's impatience and excitement over the mystery of the cave and the old man were beginning to get the best of him. He saw that he had no choice, but to go along with everything ... he certainly wasn't going anywhere else, he thought to himself, sarcastically.

"All right!" Zook announced loudly. "Let's get out of here, before you drive me crazy with your infernal questions."

As they walked, Zook filled the time with teaching. He told Zevon that the mind was given to each of us to observe and analyze the material planes. The heart or, if you prefer, the soul, was given to us so that we can travel beyond this material plane.

Zevon glanced over at Zook many times as they walked along and his questioning expression told Zook he was ready to hear more. So Zook went on with his teaching. He told Zevon that all thought is actually higher energy and the highest energies come from the imagination and the heart. "That is why you must learn to feel, Zevon. Thinking is relative to the immediate place where you are, but feeling can reach all the way into eternity."

Zevon allowed that to sink in and then he asked, "Please. Would you teach me to do these things, Zook?"

"I would be happy to teach you about them, Zevon, but you must realize something very important. I cannot do them for you. You must desire these things with all your heart and this cannot be done, unless you first begin by keeping your heart open."

"What does that mean?" asked Zevon.

"It means, my friend, that you must judge no one nor anything. You must learn to trust that everything is perfect where you are and all is perfect with what is happening during every moment." Zook explained gently, like a father to a child.

"But, Zook, that is so hard to do!" Zevon said out of sheer frustration.

"Yes, at first, it is." Zook agreed, understanding Zevon's frustration, "but isn't it true that nothing is worth having if it comes to us too easily? Do you know, Zevon, that if your heart was more fully opened, I wouldn't even need to be here, teaching you. If your heart was opened, your awareness would lead you to the cave and I wouldn't have to steer you away from possible hazards. I am here so that in moments of weakness you do not stumble and fall into trouble and thus fail to reach your destination.

You have chosen the path of heart, Zevon, and because you have, everything that happens from here on will eventually lead you to your goal. Even when it appears to you that you are failing. Understand that failure only leads to recognition of illusions that you have held onto."

Zevon felt very vulnerable and close to tears. He had never realized that all of his suffering had a purpose. "I think I understand what you are saying, Zook. If I hadn't lived in a world where feelings were shut off, then I wouldn't have known my uniqueness or the true importance of having feelings."

It had been several hours since Zook and Zevon left their camp and Zevon was glad Zook was with him, because the terrain had become terribly rough and treacherous. There were huge rocks and boulders and nearly invisible holes and deep ruts to find their way around. Zook said he knew of a path that cut through the swamp so he and Zevon were able to avoid much of the stagnant water and mud. It was hot in the swamp and there were several species of bugs to contend with. Because Zook had a reptilian skin, the heat and insects didn't bother him as much as they did Zevon.

Night was soon approaching, and Zook suggested that they find some shelter and rest for the evening. Zook knew of some caves not too far away that were heated with steam coming up from fissures deep inside the planet. He suggested they stay there for the night. The caves would be both safe and warm, so they set off walking in the direction Zook was pointing.

The swamp had been safe during the day, with the exception of the biting insects and the treacherous sand pits; however, at night there were all kinds of nocturnal creatures roaming the swamp and Zook told Zevon that some were known for being flesh eaters. The Garon were especially dangerous, Zook informed him.

"What, or who, are the Garon?" Zevon asked.

"The Garon, said Zook, are large amphibious creatures that live in the swamp. They only come out at night to feed. They're bigger than even I am and very primitive in nature. They only know two things, and they do both of them very well: eat and sleep."

When they had found the heated caves, they chose one with a narrow opening to discourage intruders. The cave overlooked the path they had taken and would afford them the best possible view to watch for the Garon.

Zook showed Zevon where to sit and sleep to keep warm and to avoid being burned by the steam that erupted occasionally from the cave floor. It had been a long day of walking and evading the many obstacles in their way. It had also been extremely tiring, wading through the swamp, and both were exhausted.

Zevon still wanted to talk a little longer, and he asked Zook if he would mind. Zook told him it would be all right, but not for long. "Please tell me again, why you are doing this for me. I want to understand." Zevon said.

"Doing what?" Zook asked, bewildered...

Zevon shook his head. "Helping me to find the cave."

Zook then told Zevon that helping him, as well as helping others, was necessary for his growth. "You see, my friend, there was a time when I hated your kind and I even killed them. I was a warrior in my race and I'd seen many battles, but my heart ached for peace and love. I yearned for a fuller and happier life, but there was so much hate in me, especially after seeing what your kind did to our planet.

Many years ago, I was a wanderer on this planet, just like you, until the old man found me and taught me. He
told me that my last test would come one day when I would find a young man from Mauldron and guide him to a cave. I was not happy to hear the young man would be from the race that I hated for so long. I was told this young man would need my compassion and my help."

Zevon was again overcome by emotion and close to tears. I must be that young man, he thought to himself. He had never had such a caring friend among his own race or felt so much love, and here it was coming from a total stranger. He smiled at Zook and said, "I love you, Zook."

Zook smiled and said, "I love you too, my friend. Now, it's time to go to sleep."

Chapter IX: Zook Says Goodbye

It was early morning when Zook woke Zevon up and told him to be very still and quiet. "The Garon are just outside the cave. While their sense of smell is poor, their hearing is excellent." Zook motioned for Zevon to walk carefully to the entrance and peek outside the cave. Zevon could not believe his eyes. He had thought at one time that Zook was ugly. These creatures were horrible and more than twice the size of Zook.

Zook, sensing some of Zevon's thoughts, whispered quietly, "They may look somewhat like me, my friend, but trust me. They have no compassion. They are only powerful savage beasts."

Suddenly, steam came shooting up from the floor and Zevon screamed. A small fissure was directly beneath his feet and he hadn't seen it. "Run!" Zook screamed. "Run for your life, Zevon!" Zevon's heart felt like it would explode as he ran deeper and deeper into the dark recesses of the cave. He ran so fast and so far that he didn't realize that Zook wasn't behind him.

"Zook!" yelled Zevon, "where are you?" It was quiet, except for Zevon's heaving breathing. No answer came. He decided to go back out to the mouth of the cave and see what had happened to Zook.

Slowly he headed back, trying to remember which turns he had taken in his haste. He finally reached the spot where Zook had screamed for him to run. Seeing no one anywhere, he yelled again. There still was no reply. Carefully, Zevon crawled out of the cave entrance and headed towards the swamp where the Garon came from. There he found what he most deeply feared.

Zook lay half in and half out of the water, covered in blood. Beside him was a Garon that Zook managed to kill at the expense of his own life. Zevon's heart was broken. He sobbed as he leaned over Zook's torn body. He had fought the Garon to give Zevon time to escape. Suddenly, a faint whisper called to Zevon from his friend's mangled body. It was barely audible. He was not dead!

"Zevon, get out of here! Now!"

"I cannot leave you, Zook, "Zevon said between great sobs. Zevon pulled on Zook's broken body, but he was just too heavy to move.

"You must go. Other Garon will come when they realize that one of their own is missing."

Zook looked at Zevon with his eyes brimming with love and compassion. "I love you, Zevon, but my time has come. You must go on to fulfill your heart's desire. I must also go to mine. I have learned to give love to those which I once hated and I am now free to leave this prison of a planet. This is just as the old man told me it would be. I am not afraid."

While Zook uttered his last words, a hideous roar came from the brush from beyond his left side. Zevon was in a panic. Zook gasped, "Run Zevon, hurry and save yourself."

Zevon, his heart pounding, looked vigorously for somewhere to run and hide. Then it hit him that the only safe place where he could go was back into the cave. The cave was large enough for Zevon, but the Garon would have to stoop down to be able to move inside the cave. He ran with all his might and, just as the Garon were closing in on him, the cave came into view. Even despite the cramped space, the Garon were able to chase Zevon deep into the cave, farther than he had been with Zook.

Suddenly, the cave floor gave way beneath Zevon's feet and he was falling. He screamed as he tumbled helplessly head over heels downward into the black depths.

Chapter X: The Keeper

With a sudden thud, Zevon hit bottom and the air was knocked out of him. Zevon was unconscious. The next thing he was aware of was a voice calling out, "Hello, hello?"

"Hello?" Zevon answered, surprised.

"It's good to see you again, Zevon." said the voice.

"Who are you, and where am I? How do you know me?" asked Zevon, amazed. The voice assured Zevon that he would be okay and that he had temporarily left his body again. Zevon struggled to gain a better awareness of his inquisitor. He could hear the voice, but he was having trouble seeing the being behind it.

"Oh stop struggling, Zevon, and you will settle into an energy of clarity." Zevon relaxed and sure enough, a form of energy began to appear before him. His heart soon recognized the features of the Keeper, whom he had seen before. His smile was so warm and peaceful, thought Zevon. "Please tell me, Zevon. What have your adventures taught you, so far?"

Zevon thought for a moment about all that had

happened over the last several days. As he recalled the events, a heavy sadness came over him.

"Zook is fine." said the voice. "Because of you, your friend was able to totally open his heart and he won't have to return to your plane again, ever."

"That's good news, Keeper. Zook became a friend and I love him. He taught me many things and I will miss him always. I've learned of my specialness, how to trust myself, and about love and friendship. What amazes me is, I've become so emotional since arriving on this planet." Zevon admitted, fresh tears in his eyes.

The voice then asked Zevon what he thought about the circumstances that led him to learn those lessons. Zevon paused for a moment to collect his thoughts and then told the Keeper, "Each situation was painful in its own way, but perfect, too, because with each experience,I learned to further open my heart."

"Excellent, Zevon," said the Keeper. "Then you also understand that without learning those lessons, you couldn't grow in your awareness or learn who you truly are. Oh, and Zevon, tears are always good. Tears are cleansing. Never be ashamed to have tears."

Zevon smiled as the Keeper's words penetrated his being and he nodded in understanding. "You always make me cry, too," Zevon told him truthfully, "but my tears with you are tears of joyous understanding, not of pain or sorrow."

The Keeper then assured Zevon that where they were could not hold pain. Only pure light and love were allowed there. The Keeper explained to Zevon that his tears now were because he was slowly remembering and awakening to the truth of his being. "You are about to experience something wonderful, Zevon. You have to remember to trust in your heart. It is time for us to part now, my friend, and it may be some time before we talk again, but I have a surprise for you."

As Zevon watched in astonishment, another light similar to the Keeper's light appeared next to him. It was made up of the same kind of energy, but it wasn't quite as intense as the Keeper's light.

"Zook!" cried Zevon in recognition. He could not believe his eyes! His heart overflowed with joy and relief.

"I have come to wish you well, my friend, and to let you know that I am fine. We will not see each other again for a while, but always remember, I am with you in your thoughts and in your heart."

Zevon smiled with a knowing that everything would be fine. As he looked at the Keeper, he felt something pull on him and he knew he was returning to his body. "Goodbye Zook. Goodbye Keeper." said Zevon. "I love you both."

Chapter XI: The Dirons

Slowly, Zevon came to consciousness in the dark place he had fallen into. It was damp and cold where he lay and there was barely any light. Suddenly, he realized he was not alone. Someone, or something, was very near him. He tentatively turned to his right and there in the dim light he saw a diminutive figure with small features and it seemed to be staring at him.

Zevon decided he'd better stand and face the stranger, but he found that he couldn't get up. "Please, help me." Zevon asked, but the being didn't answer, nor did he move, either. Each time he tried to get up, he became dizzy. Amazingly, Zevon didn't feel at all threatened as the small being stood there in the darkness. He tried again, "I'm telling you, I need your help, please! I can't seem to get up." But when he reached out to the being for help, he again lost consciousness.

Zevon slowly opened his eyes. At first, he only sensed that his body was moving. Then he saw the ceiling moving above him and he realized he was being carried. They were going through a tunnel, deeper into the cave! He finally decided that he was being carried high over the heads of his apparent rescuers, but he couldn't tell who they were, or ask where they were going. Feeling very weak and tired, and knowing he could do nothing else, Zevon fell into a deep sleep.

"Zevon," a voice called out. "Fear not. It is I, Aklar, your friend and trans dimensional teacher." Zevon could see nothing and he still wasn't sure where he was. "Rest, Zevon, you are sleeping. I'm only here to make you ready for the Dirons and to remind you again to follow your heart."

Zevon was in a restful and very submissive state. This wasn't like the energy he experienced with the Greeter. It wasn't nearly as intense or compelling. He felt no fear or need to struggle, just a resignation to listen.

"You are about to encounter a very strange people, Zevon. They're called the Dirons. They're an ancient people, cave dwellers, who have lived under Garbon for centuries. The Dirons are primitive people, but peace loving and shy of strangers. You have much to learn about them, but there's even more that you will teach them. Sleep, my friend, and then follow your heart, for it will guide you to your dream and the desires of your heart. Remember Zook and the lessons

he taught you. They will help you with the Diron."
Zevon fell back to sleep as Aklar's voice faded further
and further away.

Later, he was awakened from sleep by something wet
dripping on Zevon's face. His body was sore, but he
was more conscious than before, and there was more
light here. He was hungry. He looked around to see
where he was and he was stunned to see he was in
some kind of cell.

On further examination, he saw it was actually a
deep stone pit that he couldn't climb out of without
help.

Slowly Zevon stood. He wanted to examine the pit
some more. He soon discovered that it was made of
solid rock, both wet and very slimy. He yelled for
several minutes, but no one answered. Demoralized,
he sat back down on the wet floor and waited. Then
he saw something move. A sack was being lowered
into the pit. He couldn't see who was doing it, but he
was glad that at least someone knew he was there.

About two feet from his head, the sack was released
into his waiting arms. It contained food and a piece of
paper that looked like a message. The message was
poorly written and worded, but it seemed to say that
he must stop making any sound, because it was
harmful to their ears. Zevon considered how silly this all
seemed. It was like some childish game!

"Hello!" said a voice. Zevon got a chill down his spine.
He could hear the voice, but it was not coming from
outside of him, like a normal voice would. "We are the
Diron," the voice said again. For a moment, Zevon
thought he was losing his mind. He decided to be
silent and wait. Minutes passed and then the voice
came again.

"Don't be afraid, we will not harm you. Our method of speaking is telepathic. Sound such as yours is harmful to our ears. Please feel free to contact us in your thoughts. We will hear and we will answer."

Zevon thought again how silly this seemed! He almost spoke aloud out of habit, but he thought better of it. He decided he would try the voice's suggestion. Calming himself and stilling his emotions, he thought, "When are you getting me out of this hole?"

Surprisingly, a voice came immediately back, "When you promise to speak only in your thoughts and from your heart." Zevon laughed to himself and thought how neat this all was.

"We are a sensitive people who cannot tolerate loud noise or heavy emotion. We speak through the energies of heightened awareness that comes from our heart center. The hole you are in is not a prison, but a sound absorption chamber. It filters all loud noise and heavy emotion, so that our domain is not polluted. Do you understand?"

In his thoughts Zevon said, "I think I understand."

The voice said not to worry because they would teach and prepare him to meet with them on more comfortable terms. "You must stay in the chamber, until you have learned to balance your energies and harmonize with our nature. We mean you no harm and will take care of your physical needs. Do you understand?"

Zevon's first thought was to demand that they release him, but something inside made him relax. "Yes." said the voice in his mind.

"Good. Do not give in to fear, we will not harm you," said the voice again. If you patiently work with us we will have you out of there in no time and you will have received a great gift."

Zevon relaxed to accept his fate, for the time being, and he pondered the voice's words concerning a gift he would receive. His mind couldn't conceive what the voice was talking about, but his heart somehow quenched the impulse to give in to fear.

"Eat and then sleep," said the voice, "we will begin your training after you have eaten, rested and cleansed your energies through sleep."

Chapter XII: The Gift

"Zevon, wake up," said a voice in Zevon's mind.

"Who's there?" Zevon asked loudly, wondering where in the world he was.

"Be calm now, and remember, do not utter sounds out loud. Use your telepathy."

Zevon pulled himself together. He remembered now. He was in a sound reduction chamber where the Dirons had put him. He used his thoughts. "Okay, okay. I forgot where I was. Sorry."

The voice assured Zevon that it was okay and that time and training would make the silence a habit for him. "You probably feel, Zevon, that our methods are cruel and unjust. If you will only trust me, we shall teach you a great mystery of life." Zevon listened intently to the voice. "Do you know how I know your name?" The voice asked silently again.

Zevon thought for a minute and then realized he had spoken his name to no one. "We, the Diron, have learned to access knowledge by stilling the outer sound and opening ourselves to the inner sound -- the sound of our feelings. We know who you are, where you have come from, and we also know where you hope to go."

It entered Zevon's mind for just a millisecond that this might all be a trick. The voice responded immediately, "You are Zevon, formerly of the planet, Mauldron, and you have been abandoned here by your own people. The place you seek has a magic about it and an old man who has the answers you are searching for."

Zevon was astounded. This telepathy may be weird, but it sure wasn't a trick -- it was real. "It's no big deal, Zevon. It is our way, a way that we would like to teach you, if you will only permit us. We will not force this issue with you, Zevon. If you choose not to work with us, then we will be forced to place you back outside the cave to find your own way to the old man and his cave."

Zevon thought about what the voice was saying and he thoughtfully said through his mind that he was again sorry. He would gladly agree to the training. "I desire to know my heart and my heart's desire. To find these answers, I must travel and meet with the old man," said Zevon.

"You will meet the old man, Zevon, and you will help us to solve a problem at the same time." Spoke the voice inside Zevon's mind. "Much later on, I promise, you will understand everything. "Zevon," the voice continued, "the chamber you are in has two marvelous functions. It not only cushions sound from contaminating our domain, it can also create a doorway to infinite inner worlds." Zevon was amazed.

"It can convert outer sound into a vehicle by which you can ride the energy to wherever you want to go.

We are not affected by your sounds, unless we venture too close to the edge of the pit, because the pit completely absorbs all negative and emotionally charged energy. The pit is composed of a very rare rock known as Heartite. It is known in other galaxies as soul stone." The voice paused. "Do you know why this is, Zevon?"

Using telepathy more easily now, Zevon admitted to the voice that he had never heard of this stone, but he believed what the voice was telling him was true. He had no reason not to believe. "My friends, Zook and The Greeter, told me that I can always trust my heart and feelings."

The voice responded, "What is your heart telling you now, Zevon?"

Zevon replied, "It tells me that you are honest and telling me the truth."

There was a pause. "Very good, my friend, you are learning." said the voice. "Zevon, the pit, as I said, absorbs negative thoughts, but it also amplifies positive thoughts. If you were to focus, for a moment, on one positive thought, it would magnify itself in intensity by a thousand-fold. Any thought, Zevon, can be amplified in the pit to the point where that one thought becomes a reality." The voice paused again, giving Zevon a chance to absorb so much new information. "Do you understand what I have just said?"

Zevon thought it over for a moment. "You mean that this pit helps one open their heart to greater awareness. Right?"

The voice replied, "It's so much more than that, Zevon. The pit allows you to transport your awareness to wherever you want to go -- and it will also take your body, if you choose to."

Zevon said "Wow!"

"Any obstacles you may encounter, Zevon, are but opportunities to increase your inner awareness and make you aware of your personal power. So many people, and entire races, do not understand that the power to overcome their problems is there within them. Rather than seek the answers from within, they pout, become angry and frustrated, and they shut down this marvelous gift. All of the obstacles are merely love's way of leading you home to your heart."

There was a pause, and then the voice continued. "Do you understand what I'm saying to you, Zevon?"

Zevon was exhilarated by this information and replied, "Yes, I do! I really do see and understand!"

"Wonderful!" replied the voice. "You are doing very well, an excellent student! Tomorrow we shall put all of this knowledge into action."

Zevon responded, "If I'm doing so well, then will I be getting out of the pit soon?"

The voice came back immediately, but this time it was slow and gentle. "Zevon, think about all I have told you. You can leave the pit whenever you choose to. Think about all I've said, but listen with your heart, not with your mind and its pitiful reasoning abilities."

I can leave the pit when I choose? Zevon thought. It didn't make sense and he was puzzled.

The voice spoke, "Patience my friend. It is time now to sleep and rest your energies. Tomorrow will be a most interesting day for you."

Zevon woke, fairly bristling with excitement. He was anxious to learn more about the power of the pit and how it might allow him to escape his circumstances. His first thoughts were, "Hello? Is anyone there?" When there was no reply, Zevon became anxious. He thought, "Please answer me. Is anyone there?" Still there was no answer.

Zevon began to wonder if all that was happening was some sort of mind-made delusion, due to his fall. Had he really communicated telepathically to someone outside the pit?

Zevon realized he was becoming emotional again, but still he began to cry. His heart might have broken, had it not been for the strangest feeling that suddenly came over him. He recognized the presence of a similar energy he felt before, when he was with the Greeter. Suddenly, Zevon had a hunch to relax and think about his departed friend, Zook. Zevon had loved Zook and, the more he thought about the love he felt for his friend, the less sad he felt.

Zevon's chest burned slightly and a joyous peace started to fill the pit. He closed his eyes and swore he saw Zook's face smiling at him. His emotion changed from sadness to joy. New tears streamed down his face as he watched the form of Zook try to materialize before him. It was Zook all right, but his body was slightly transparent.

"Greetings, Zevon, my friend." Zook said to him.

"Zook! I'm so glad to see you!" responded Zevon.

"I have come one last time to help you," said Zook, "but you must listen to me carefully and trust what I say. Do you understand?"

Zevon replied, "I will do whatever you tell me to do, my friend."

"Great." said Zook. "Tell me, what is your greatest desire right now?"

"Zook, I want to leave this pit and continue on my journey to find the old man." Zevon told him.

"How are you going to do this, Zevon?" asked Zook.

Zevon became sad again for a moment. "I truly don't know, my friend."

"Zevon, you know how much I care. Please also know I say this to you out of love and friendship. Stop feeling sorry for yourself! You are only wasting energy and doing damage to your nervous system!" Zook exclaimed. " Zevon, pause for a moment and consider what it took to get my image here. What were your feelings and emotions, prior to my appearance?"

Zevon thought for a moment before he responded. "Well, actually, I was sad at first because I was alone. Then I was filled with incredible joy, as I thought about you and our friendship. The feelings then increased until you appeared."

"Love, Zevon. It was your love, your heart to be precise, that brought me here." Zook explained to him. "Love makes all things possible, Zevon. When you stop feeling sorry for yourself long enough to focus with intent on what you truly want, it will then appear. Zevon, I'm going to be honest with you."

"Please do, my friend. "replied Zevon.

"You tend to expect the worst, at times, and because you do, you get it. But that's okay, because you are learning that it is a choice and not an absolute. You will soon discover that all obstacles are merely tests for you -- tests to teach you to uncover your power and your true nature. Love where you are, Zevon, and this will reveal the means for escape. Love who you are and you will be able to escape anytime you want to. Do you understand, my dear friend?" Zook asked him.

"I understand what you are saying, Zook, but not how to do what you are saying. My mind looks around at my sorry predicament and it tells me what you say can't be possible."

Zook smiled at Zevon and told him that he had to leave. "Don't worry, Zevon, you are not alone, but you will have to find the way out of here yourself. I am not allowed to steal this opportunity for growth away from you. As a reminder, please think back to all you have learned ... about trusting in your heart. Your heart, Zevon."

With that, the nearly transparent image of Zook slowly dissolved, just as it had appeared a short while ago. Zevon was again alone. He was left to contemplate his fate and the words of his friend. As he sat on the wet floor to rest, he caught himself dozing off and decided to lie down and get some sleep.

Chapter XIII: Passing The Test

Zevon awoke confused. He wasn't at first aware of the day or the time since he had been put in the pit. Time had escaped him and the only thing that he knew he wanted, or that really mattered, was getting out. He battled the impulse to be angry at his situation. He realized that fear was not the problem, because he knew that he was not alone. This thought brought him comfort and gratitude.

Surrounded by good feelings, he then noticed that his heart burned with a growing warmth and peace that he couldn't fully comprehend. This allowed him to work within the energy of the pit. He thought about all he had learned from his teachers, and with that came a great surge of confidence, which he had never felt before. It was like an assurance that something wonderful was about to happen.

Zevon's excitement only grew as he basked in the emotions and flowing energy around him. He had never felt so free before. He was no longer lying in a pool of self-pity. He was beginning to realize that he could control his thoughts, no matter what the challenge was that he faced!

What excited Zevon most was the feeling of complete, total freedom that he was approaching. It was like being transported to another place. He struggled with that for what seemed hours, but the more he tried, the weaker he became and finally he had to give up and rest. Zevon wondered what it would take to find the key that would set him free. He was happy about the day's discoveries, but he still felt something important was missing.

"Zevon?" a voice said. This time, it was not the voice of Zook, the Diron, or even the Greeter. Still, he knew this voice. He was sure it was someone he knew.

"Who are you?" thought Zevon, using his telepathy.

"It's me, Xela. Do you remember me, Zevon?"

"Xela!" Zevon said excitedly. "Why did you leave, like you did?"

Xela then explained that she had no choice. He needed to experience some things that she was unable to teach him. "I wanted to help you, Zevon, but it would not have worked out the right way. You must learn as much as you can on your own, or you will not fully realize who you truly are."

"Help me get out of here, Xela," Zevon pleaded. "I don't know how I know , but you can help me, I just know it."

Xela told Zevon that it was not necessary for her to help him because he was fully capable of getting out on his own. "You already know how to do that, Zevon! Remember, you must trust in your heart."

Frustrated, Zevon asked Xela if there was anything she could do that would help.

"No, I cannot get you out of the pit, Zevon. Only you can do that, but I will show you how to touch a deeper part of your power where you can leave the pit and go wherever you want."

Zevon was thrilled. "When can we start?"

"As soon as you wish, Zevon," she told him. "You must do exactly as I tell you and, in the way that I tell you to do it. Do you understand me, Zevon?" Xela asked.

Zevon answered her, "Yes. I understand."

Xela then told him to sit down and to completely relax. He was to put everything out of his mind and, above all else, open his heart and begin to feel. "Can you sense the energy of the pit, Zevon?" She asked.

"Yes, it has an uplifting effect that I've noticed when I'm relaxed," Zevon told her.

"You must become one with that energy, Zevon. That is what will take you out of the pit," she said. "Do not try to analyze or think about it. You must feel it in your heart. Can you do that?"

Zevon acknowledged that he understood and he said he was beginning to feel a sense of joy and freedom growing inside him.

"Good. Now, close your eyes. Imagine things as you would like them to be. Do not think them into your mind, but allow your imagination to paint a beautiful picture of the way you would like things to be. You may even see me in your mind, if that will help."

Zevon released all expectations and judgment of what he wanted and pictured it in his mind. Slowly, the images became real enough to walk into. He could see Xela, as well as some strange little people standing around her that looked very familiar to Zevon.

Xela motioned for him to come to her. That surprised him. He didn't expect the images to move. With a force of will and desire, Zevon walked in his mind towards Xela. It was difficult at first, like trying to run in water or move under the influence of a drug. Slowly, everything around him became quite normal and he was with Xela and the little people.

"Do not speak, Zevon. Like me, use your telepathy. Remember, your thoughts can be heard by everyone and the sound is painful for them," she explained.

Zevon was elated! He smiled as he looked into Xela's childlike face. She was beautiful! He had not had time to talk to her the last time, and his mind held a thousand questions. She motioned for him to follow her and they walked out of the dark chamber into a large area of greater light.

As they moved into the light, Zevon noticed that the little people had no eyes. Xela told him not to be concerned, because they had learned over the years to trust their heart and feelings. They didn't worry about their lack of sight.

Chapter XIV: The Choice

Zevon and Xela walked for a while, until they came to an underground chamber loaded with clear rocks. She motioned for him to sit with her in the center of the chamber. The little people didn't follow them, but remained outside in the tunnel.

"Zevon, can you feel my thoughts?" she asked. Zevon nodded. He could, and he marveled at the ease of communicating in this manner, without moving his mouth. "I need to talk to you seriously for a moment," she told him. "Do you understand me?"

Zevon smiled and, through his thoughts, he told her he understood and would listen.

"You've come a long way in your journey to find your heart and you're about to reach your destination. You'll have a choice to make soon that will affect your journey and it's outcome. I can't tell you the right choice to make, but I wanted to make you aware of it. Your soul will testify to it when it's presented to you.

Okay, Zevon?" Xela asked him.

In his thoughts, Zevon said, "Okay, but I want to know if you are coming with me."

Xela smiled at Zevon and said she would gladly meet him after he had found her grandfather in the land of Ohah. "I cannot go with you, Zevon. This is something you must do on your own. All you have learned about yourself, up to now, has prepared you well for entrance into my grandfather's land. Remember to keep your heart open and do not judge. Your heart will guide you always."

Zevon noticed that the chamber was filled with an intense feeling of well-being and peace. The clear rocks that lined the chamber even felt like they were alive. In a way he could not explain, Zevon knew he could talk to them, if he wanted to. Xela, too, had a warm and lovely glow about her that only endeared her more to Zevon's heart. For the first time, he realized he was in love with her and he didn't want to leave her.

"Close your eyes, Zevon, and empty your mind. Think of nothing. Be still in the silence. When you have done this, let
 your imagination create whatever comes to mind and don't judge it." she said. "This energy is here to encourage you and remind you of the joy that is to come. Ohah is a beautiful land and the doorway to infinity."

Zevon did as she requested and he was surprised at how quickly images began to appear in his mind. He could see a beautiful place where all manner of creatures and beings came to him. Some even spoke words of love and encouragement to him through their thoughts. Finally, an old man appeared. He was grey-haired and wearing a long violet robe and leather sandals.

When the old man saw Zevon, he smiled and reached over to touch him on his heart. Zevon was stunned. He felt incredible warmth radiating from his chest where the old man touched him and this warmth traveled to all parts of his being. He had felt this energy before, but now he was able to consciously enjoy it and experience it with all of his senses. Before, he had either been asleep or unconscious when he experienced this.

For the first time, Zevon realized everything that everyone had been trying to teach him. He was not a prisoner of circumstances, or of an unkind fate. He was simply wherever his mind chose to be. His obstacles were illusions that matched his beliefs and he was only a prisoner, if he perceived himself to be one.

Again Zevon focused on the old man in his mind. He spoke to Zevon through his thoughts and told him that they would meet soon. Zevon asked him if he was Xela's grandfather. The old man smiled and nodded that indeed he was.

"Follow your heart, Zevon. It will lead you to me and to all that your heart desires," said the old man. With that said, he vanished from Zevon's mind.

Zevon was thrilled with what was happening. He opened his eyes, wanting to share his experiences with Xela, but she was gone. Just like before, she had disappeared without a word! Why was it that every time he was about to get to know her better, she slipped out of his life? Then he heard her voice in his mind, "Remember, Zevon, I will see you when you reach the cave at Ohah where my grandfather is."

Zevon felt like staying in the chamber for awhile, but he knew that he had to move on. The energy in the room was dwindling and he still had to find Ohah. He left the chamber of the clear rocks and walked back out into the tunnel that Xela had led him through. There in the shadows, he met a small group of Dirons. The little people smiled at him and using his telepathy, he thanked them for taking care of him. He told them he forgave them for putting him in the pit because what they taught him was well worth any frustration.

One of the Diron people asked Zevon if they could ask a favor before he left. Zevon said it would be all right. "We want to go with you to Ohah." said the little being. "We need your eyes for the journey and you will need our feelings to guide you to Ohah."

Zevon was reluctant at first, but then he listened to his heart. It told him that bringing the Diron people along would be okay, and he truly could use their help. In fact, Zevon had no idea where to begin the journey and asked the little people to give him directions. Zevon was stunned when they told him they didn't know the way to Ohah either. They told him they must return to the chamber and search their feelings for the answer. Zevon agreed to go along, and he and the little people went back inside.

Once they were back in the chamber, they sat in a huge circle and, in their thoughts and feelings, each requested the greater part of their inner being to give them guidance to Ohah. It was beautiful! The energy again began to rise until it filled the chamber with warmth and brotherly love that overflowed in their hearts. They all knew, at once, that each was to help the other, and there would be strength in doing so.

Zevon again saw images of beings, while visions of comfort and love were also shown to him. He could

feel the energy and this brought him great delight. Finally, the smiling old man reappeared and motioned for Zevon to follow him.

Together, they walked through magnificent crystal hallways, until they came, at last, to the most beautiful clearing Zevon had ever seen. It was full of trees and flowers, and there were different types of animals all about. Zevon could hardly believe the wonders he was seeing!

Way beyond the clearing, he could see an impressive mountain range of pure crystal, but towering way up and through the clouds in the sky. The energy in the clearing was incredible, almost magical, in its essence. Zevon felt that he could do anything. As if the old man had heard him, he suggested that Zevon think about being in the crystal mountains. Suddenly, they both were in the mountains! Zevon felt like a child again.

There was an incredible glowing light coming from the mountains and it seemed to come mainly from one peak very close to where they were. The old man motioned for Zevon to walk towards the light. Zevon asked in his thoughts whether the old man was coming, too. He smiled and said he would not.

Zevon walked towards the light and, with each step, his eagerness grew. There was mystery and magic in that light and Zevon sensed that the answers he was looking for would also be there. As he got closer, he could see a golden door right at the very center of it. There were some words carved into the wood of the door, but he couldn't quite make them out from where he was. The closer he got to the door, the more apparent it became that the words were in some foreign language he didn't understand.

Zevon turned for the first time to ask the old man for help in reading what was on the door, but the old man was gone and so were the mountains. Zevon found himself alone in front of a shining golden door, not knowing whether he could (or even should) open it. Somehow, he intuitively felt the strange words had something to do with what was on the other side of the door.

Darkness surrounded him like a dense black fog. This made him feel uneasy, but each time he looked at the golden door, his heart felt warm inside. He decided to try and open it.

"Don't touch me!" shouted the door. Zevon was shaken by the unexpected voice.

"Who are you?" Zevon asked, incredulously.

"You don' t know who I am?" the door answered.

Zevon could only shake his head in wonder. "How could I know you? I've never met you before."

"Do you mean to say, you've read me, and yet you still choose to ignore the words on the front of me?" asked the door.

"I didn't read them because I don't understand the language in which they're written! I decided to open you anyway." Zevon confessed to the door.

"You will have to go back then. You will not be able to open me until you've learned their meaning."

Zevon was dumbfounded. He couldn't believe this. It was crazy! A talking door -- a door giving orders!

Then a gentle hand was placed on his shoulder. He turned to see who it was and there stood Xela, smiling at him. She said not to worry, because he would soon learn the meaning of the words on the door and be able to open it. "But for now, you must go back to the little people, the Diron people, and help them to find the entrance to Ohah. It lays buried deep within the planet and the long path there is dangerous. That's why they need your eyes." Xela told him.

Zevon felt a warm and gentle tenderness as he looked into Xela's clear blue eyes." I love you, Xela. You must know that I do" he admitted to her, openly.

"I know you do, Zevon. I have felt your love in my heart, but the time for us isn't now. We will have our time together when you reach Ohah. First, though, you must reach Ohah. I hope you understand."

He smiled back, feeling also what was in her heart. Then he told her he understood. He knew he should finish his journey, before he could share anything enduring with her. Xela reached up to hold him gently by the shoulders and she sweetly kissed his cheek.

With a loud gasp, Zevon came back to consciousness. All around him, crowded the little people asking telepathically if he was okay. He told them he was just fine and that he had been on a wonderful journey within. "I know what we must do." he told them.

Zevon then gathered the Diron people around him and told them he was going to find the entrance to Ohah. He asked if they still wanted to go with him. Each of the little people, in turn, responded that they wished to go along.

Chapter XV: The Door of Ohah

There was a legend among the people of Garbon that deep within the planet existed a mystical door called the Door of Ohah. It was said to be a magical door, through which those who were worthy could escape to other dimensions and times. No one had ever laid claim to seeing it, for those who left seeking it never returned.

Garbon's interior was full of tunnels that ran deep into the planet, a planet which was mostly carbon and volcanic ash. Garbon's center was very hot with thousands of fissures functioning as steam geysers to relieve the pressure from the core. If one could not discern which tunnel to travel through, they could be boiled alive. Oxygen was plentiful enough, but there was also sulfur to contend with and it could become unbearable, at times.

The trip to Ohah would be extremely dangerous. Not even the underground inhabitants of Garbon, the Diron, were completely sure the legend of the Door to Ohah was even true, let alone that a path to the legendary door even existed. No one they knew had ever been there.

Zevon was about to get another surprise. He wasn't aware that the Diron that were present actually represented only a handful of the population that composed their race. All totaled, there were just over 6,000 Dirons living in their kingdom. Zevon had never dreamed that he would be escorting more than 6,000 elflike beings to the distant place he was traveling to! "Where are all the others, then?" he asked those who were present. They responded that the rest were hiding in various tunnels and chambers a good ways away from where they now stood.

Chapter XVI: The Chamber of Light

The Diron escorted Zevon out of the chamber and into a large underground amphitheater. Zevon had not realized one was so close. It was huge! The amphitheater had to be nearly a mile in circumference and it was lit and heated by various volcanic fires from deep within the planet that peeped through holes in the floor.

The apparent leader of the Diron was already speaking to his people, although Zevon was unable to see him, or the audience, at first. Slowly, from other holes in the floor and walls, Zevon watched as little heads began to pop up. Zevon was amused at the sight, as he considered the Diron to be both cute in a way, and yet also very homely in their outer appearance.

He was told that Zir was the name of their leader. Zir of the Diron spoke: "Brothers and Sisters, this is a wonderful day for our people. Into our hands, the universe has sent a being from another planet and race to guide us to the Door of Ohah. Through his eyes, we will know where to step and thus avert many dangers and the loss of many lives."

Voices called out telepathically from within the crowd, wanting to know who this being was and asking whether he could be trusted. Zir spoke to his people again, reassuring them that this being could indeed be trusted. Then, to Zevon's surprise, Zir turned to introduce him and ask him to speak.

Zevon took a deep breath to gather his courage and open his heart, and walked forward to address the Diron population. "People of Diron," Zevon sent through his mind, " I am an outcast on this planet. I'm seeking to escape my former circumstances and find the meaning of my life. I was rejected by my people and condemned to stay here until I changed my ways. My path has been dangerous and because of my blindness of heart, I have paid a high price. Because of you I have learned to trust myself and the power of my inner being. I have learned to feel with my heart and I speak to you now without vocal sounds, just as you have taught me. I am indebted to you for this gift and I ask that you trust me, as we all seek the same thing."

Zevon felt good inside for what he had just said. As he looked out into the sea of faces, their smiles greeted him from all sides. Smiles without eyes. A feeling of love and comradeship came over him. This was something he never expected.

Zir spoke to him. "Thank you, Zevon. My heart has told me you can be trusted with our lives and if the others all agree, then we will accompany you on this journey of discovery."

Zir then turned to the crowd. "My people, I ask that you take into your hearts the words of this being and, in so doing, realize he is a brother and worthy of trust."

There was a long and protracted pause and then total silence. The wait was hard for Zevon, since he was anxious to have their answer. Zevon tried looking into their faces for a clue, but it was difficult to read the Diron, because their lack of eyes hid their intentions.

Suddenly, as Zevon watched, the Diron rose from their seats and began to move into a gigantic circular formation. Holding hands, they started to hum in unison. Zevon felt a burning in his heart, as the low humming increased in tempo and became a loud deep vibration. All at once, he felt the floor give way beneath him. To his surprise, he was rising into the air above the floor.

Zir spoke to him telepathically and told him not to be afraid. It was his people's way of showing Zevon that they trusted and believed in him. The Diron had learned to use a very low frequency vibration to move and shape matter. The deep humming vibration was a form of mass visualization which could be used both constructively and destructively, if need be. Zir told Zevon that he had yet one other surprise for him. "We will not be without guidance on our journey. The people have decided to trust you with their hearts and their lives. They have also chosen to reveal to you their guardian, Shema.

Shema was a being who had crept into the imaginations of all the Diron over the centuries. Shema sounded like a God or a spirit to Zevon, but Zir assured him Shema was neither. She is a being of light who has guided our people for centuries. Zir said Shema had told them of his coming.

Chapter XVII: Shema

The humming began again, just as Zir ended his talk with Zevon. As Zevon watched, a pink glowing light began to appear in the epicenter of the gigantic circle where the people held hands. Zevon hadn't felt such an incredible energy since he got out of the pit with Xela's help.

The glowing light became even brighter pink and was about a foot in diameter. Zevon noticed there were smiles of joy on the Diron faces and tears on others. It was if they could see the being that was materializing. Slowly, the ball of light took form and a person began to emerge.

The form was Xela! She motioned to Zevon not to say anything. She smiled and walked towards him. "I'm glad you are going to help them, Zevon, and because you are, I will be assisting you on the journey." she told him. "My pink essence will help you, if you get lost, but I am not permitted to find the Door of Ohah for you.

You must find it yourself, with them.   Understand?"

"Yes, I understand." he said. "When can I see you again?"

"You can see me whenever you wish, after you have found and passed through the Door of Ohah." replied Xela with a smile. "Which way does your heart tell you to go right now?" Xela asked him.

Zevon stopped looking at her and closed his eyes. He felt the question within his heart. He said it felt like the passage was just beyond the flames, over in the distance. He pointed in that direction. Yes, he felt in it in his heart. That was the way to go. Xela smiled and said he was right.

"You're trusting your heart, Zevon, this is good. It will never, ever lie to you." she reassured him. With that, she walked back into the center of the circle and began to glow bright pink once again. Then she turned into a ball of brilliant pink light and was gone.

Chapter XVIII: The Journey Within

Zir spoke to his people and asked if they were ready to begin the journey. They all nodded in unison that they were willing and ready to begin. He looked at Zevon and smiled. Zevon took Zir's hand and instructed the others to hold the hand of the person next to them. Slowly then, the army of lost souls walked beyond the flames and into an uncharted maze of tunnels that hopefully would soon lead to the Door of Ohah and their freedom.

The tunnels were wet and slimy with growths of moss and mildew covering the walls on either side. The tunnels were large enough to walk in, but you had to be careful of fissures in the floor and steam that came up abruptly from some of them. Zevon painstakingly guided the little people and carefully passed all information back through the long snaking line about which was the safest way to go and about the various objects to avoid along their path.

They had already walked for several hours in the tunnels through the bowels of the planet when Zevon noticed a clearing up ahead. His first thought was whether this may be the land of Ohah in the distance.

Coming in to the clearing, he could see that the ceiling was made of pure crystal and had to be several miles in circumference. Right in front of him was a bridge that was very old and the path actually went over it leading to a door at the base of a mountain. He again wondered whether this could possibly be the door at the entrance of Ohah.

As they crossed over the bridge and got closer to the door, Zevon felt strangely uncomfortable. He felt cold and an uneasy feeling permeated his whole being. This door did not look anything like the door he encountered in his vision with the old man. This door was large and covered with dying vegetation and gnarled old vines, and it looked like it hadn't been opened in centuries.

The Diron, sensing Zevon's stress, asked if he was all right. Zevon told them about the door and said there was something written on it that he wouldn't be able to read until he got closer.

Chapter XIX: The Door of Death

Zevon went to the huge door on the side of the mountain in the clearing. With his hand, he brushed away the cobwebs and pushed away the vegetation and vines covering the words. He still couldn't read the inscription. Like in his vision, it was in another language, one that he didn't understand. He tried to describe to Zir the nature of the symbols and hieroglyphics, but Zir wasn't familiar with the language either.

Suddenly, a deep male voice came out of nowhere, "I can tell you what the words mean."

Zevon jumped in surprise and nervously looked around for the person who spoke. Then out of the bushes a figure emerged and walked towards them. The being was very tall and wore a black robe with a hood that totally concealed his face. He held a wooden staff with a stone of some sort on the very top of it in his right hand. There was an eeriness about the being and Zevon felt a sudden cold chill. Even his motions were strange. He seemed to float towards them, rather than walk, and the closer he came, the more Zevon's heart and senses warned him to beware.

"My name is Gall," said the being in that same deep voice. "Who might you be?"

"My name is Zevon, and these are the Diron." he replied, indicating the huge throng of little people with his extended arm.

"Where do you think you are going?" Gall asked in that same rude tone.

"We are on a journey. We seek the door to the entrance of Ohah." Zevon answered.

"The Door of Ohah!" laughed the robed being. "Why that is a fable as old as this planet is. No one has ever found that door, because it doesn't exist!" boasted the being sarcastically.
"We will find it." Zevon told him, nervously.

"Boy, do you have any idea what it says on this door?" Gall asked him in the same rude tone.

"No," Zevon said, "but it doesn't matter, because we won't stop searching until we've found it."

"Let me read it to you then."

"YOU ARE NOW ON THE LAND OF GAR. HE WHO TRESPASSES HERE AND TRAVELS BEYOND THIS DOOR WILL DIE."

"Who is Gar?" asked Zevon.

"Who is Gar?" exclaimed the being angrily, "Gar is the oldest being on this planet. Some say he is a sorcerer who delights in sacrificing all manner of creatures to his dark friends. This door is the last and only warning you will get."

"I'm sure we can reason with Gar or maybe we can even find a way around this door." Zevon told him.

"Reason with Gar? "laughed the being again, seeming to enjoy this like it was a game. "Gar doesn't reason, boy. He wants and needs blood. If you and your friends choose to persist beyond this door, you will most certainly die."

With that, Gall quickly turned and floated back into the bushes, laughing and shrieking like a mad man.

Zevon followed him, but when he tried to enter the bushes, he found no sign of anyone there and no sign of any passageway through. The mysterious being who had called himself Gall had disappeared and was nowhere to be seen.

Zevon returned to the door, sensing that the Diron were upset and confused. He took hold of Zir's hand

and asked what was the matter. Using his mind, Zir told Zevon that the people were afraid and most of them wanted to go back. Zevon spoke to the people then and reminded them of what their life had been like in the cave of tunnels. He asked if they were sure they wanted to live the rest of their lives underground like frightened animals.

"I will not let Gar harm any of you. I swear this on my life." Zevon promised. Suddenly, the rhythmic humming began again and Zevon knew that he had reached them. The people would follow him.

At that moment, he knew something instinctively about the door. He had sensed through his heart that the door could be opened by using a combination of sounds along with words.

Zevon walked back across the open area to where the door was. He had this strange feeling he was to utter what had entered his mind at that moment. He opened his mouth and spoke the words KEE-SO-MAH out loud, but very slowly drawn out and with intent. The door moved, but only slightly.

Then Zevon got the idea to ask the Diron to assist him. Maybe there was power in the strength of the number of voices! Unaccustomed to making sounds, they all agreed to go along with Zevon's wishes.

All joined in saying the word. This time, to the amazement of everyone, the door opened with a jarring, creaking motion. Before them was a long corridor that was dimly lit and beyond that, they could only assume, lay the land of Gar.

Chapter XX: The Land of Gar

Slowly, Zevon and the Diron walked down the long corridor towards the light, which appeared as a bright dot ahead of them. Zevon was amazed at the smoothness of the floor and walls. It was if they had been cut out and sanded smooth by a laser. His heart began to beat louder than usual, he noticed. He couldn't help wondering what might happen and if this Gar was really as horrible as the strange being had warned.

From the door where they entered, it appeared that the tunnel was not too long, but they had walked for a while now, and it was becoming quite apparent that they would be walking even longer. Zevon thought about Xela and how incredible his life had become since he left his planet. No one on Mauldron would ever have believed this, not in a thousand years! How wonderful it was to discover that feeling different from everyone else all his life was actually a good thing. He was just as he should be. It was so simple and so amazing, he thought. All you have to do is trust in your heart and all your dreams will come true.

Suddenly, Zevon looked up, only to realize that the light they had been heading towards was gone. He was also shaken by the familiar voice they heard when they were outside the door, the one that seemed to come from nowhere -- Gall.

"Didn't listen, did you, boy?"

He quickly turned around to see if he could see where the voice was coming from. He could see nothing but the long chain of Diron people. Then Gall began his haunting laugh that faded out into an eerie stillness.

Zir telepathically told Zevon not to worry. He felt Gall

was merely playing mind games with them, and trying to scare them so they would turn around and leave. Zevon thanked Zir for his support and looked into the distance again. He couldn't understand where the dot of light at the end of the corridor had gone.

As they walked, Zevon stared down the corridor, and as they got closer, he realized the light was actually still there, but something was in front of the light, partially blocking it's source. Closer and closer they walked, while Zevon strained his eyes, trying to make out what was blocking the light, and the passage to whatever lay beyond the light. Suddenly, Zevon knew. As strange as it seemed, he recognized Anggar -- and he knew Anggar was dead.

Anggar's huge body was draped over the hole as a gruesome warning. Zevon made the decision not to tell the Diron about Anggar. It would only frighten them and, besides, it was only a warning at this point.

Zir asked if there was a problem, but Zevon told him there was a blockage in their path, a rock and some other debris, but he could clear it away. He wondered for a moment whether Xela was all right, but his heart told him that she was okay.

Zevon was so taken aback by the sight of his poor friend as he removed him from the opening, that he didn't at first notice the enormous underground world Anggar's body was hiding from view.

Once they crossed through the portal, light was everywhere, just as they entered the opening. Zevon couldn't believe his eyes. Here they were, miles underground, and yet it was like being on the planet's surface. There was what looked like a sky here, from the reflection off of a gigantic luminous rock somewhere, and miles and miles of dense forest.

Mountains towered high off in the distance, and Zevon noticed one mountain in particular that stood out, much higher than the rest. It had a cap on the top of it that looked like a skull in terrible pain. Zevon's heart sank with fear as he focused on it. He thought to himself that the mountain must be Gar's place. He was glad the Diron people couldn't see this land for it was not inviting to the eyes -- nor the heart.

It was at this point that Zevon sought guidance from Xela for the first time. He closed his eyes and, as he had learned to do, he allowed his heart to recall her image as vividly as possible in his imagination. His heart began to burn as he felt her energy. He opened his eyes and there was her pink essence pointing, just like a finger, towards the skulled mountain.
Zevon decided it would be a good time to rest for awhile. He felt tired, but they were underground and he couldn't tell if it was day or night up on the surface. Zevon also felt the Diron people would welcome a rest. Besides, it was time he told the truth about what was happening.

When they walked down the mountainside to a clearing, he let Zir know they would rest here and regain their strength. He also told Zir he needed to address the people about what was ahead, for it could become dangerous.

The Diron formed their circle in the clearing and prepared to hear Zevon's words. It must be a strange sight, a young boy surrounded by more than 6,000 eyeless little people, thought Zevon. It was a big responsibility, there was no doubt about that. But he also realized how important they were to him. He needed to talk to them about Gar and he knew, somehow, that their powers were going to be very important to all of them, if there was trouble.

Zevon took a deep breath and stood. Then he began to update the people about what had happened since they first entered the tunnel. He also told them about Anggar. Many became afraid, but the majority remained strong and vowed to stand by Zevon, even if there was a fight.

Zir told Zevon it was important to keep the people in dim light, because their powers were diminished by bright light. He said that they felt okay, but Zir could tell they had come to a lighter environment. He cautioned Zevon that if they remained in bright light for too long, the people would become weak and go into a sleep of no return. Zevon thanked Zir for this information and he asked the people to rest for awhile.

Looking at the skull mountain, Zevon sensed that something fearful was going to happen. His eyes grew heavy and he laid on his back to rest. The luminous rock that made up the false sky seemed soothing to his mind and slowly he fell into a deep sleep.

Chapter XXI: Alone!

Zevon woke from his sleep and, for a moment, he forgot where he was and the circumstances he was in. The false sky again had such a comforting effect in such a dismal place. He rolled over to his side to see how the little people were getting along -- and they were gone! Quickly
he sat up and looked all around to see if they had merely moved. They were nowhere in sight. Panic and fear were setting in, but he touched his heart, closed his eyes, and felt the burning reassurance that he was okay.

An object caught his attention off in the distance. It appeared to be something hanging from a tree and the light flickered off of it. Zevon decided to have a closer look.

As he approached the object, his heart burned. This gave way to a chilling feeling and a heavy foreboding. It looked like it might be one of the little people, but there was no movement. Finally he realized that it was one of the Dirons and he was dead! There was a dagger with a skull on it pinning the small body to the tree.

There was a note attached to the dagger. Zevon gently pulled out the knife and the lifeless body slid to the ground. With the note grasped tightly in his fist, Zevon felt helpless but he also felt a growing resolve. How could anyone so brutally murder a helpless creature like this Diron? He felt totally alone, and yet there was something new awakening inside him. A new courage, or maybe it was determination, was growing. He was not going to let this situation stop him or end the journey they were on!

Zevon made up his mind. They had nothing to lose and everything to gain! Not even the possibility of his death bothered him anymore.

Zevon carried the body to a cave he spotted as they came down the mountain. There, he laid the small Diron to rest. It was a fitting place, he decided, since the little being had spent an entire life in a different cave, a cave he had called home. Zevon then returned to the clearing and sat under the same tree to read the note.

The note was written in large red letters:
"WE ARE WAITING FOR YOU IN THE`MOUNTAIN OF THE SKULL. THEY ARE WAITING. I AM WAITING -- FOR YOU TO DIE."

The note was signed by Gar.

Zevon was surprised to find that he was not angry. He also realized that he was not afraid. He only felt again that same growing resolve and he knew he had no choice but to try and rescue the little people. Then they would continue on to find the door. He was numb, but he also felt powerful, too. He didn't know how he was going to pull off the rescue, but death was not an issue -- that didn't bother him anymore.

Somehow, all that he had been through and seen had caused him to realize the integrity of his life. He was no longer looking at himself emotionally or only from the outside. He felt the power and integrity of who he was and this growing confidence caused him to have faith that all would be well.

A peace came over Zevon as he recognized there was a purpose to all that was happening. He couldn't put it into words, but in his heart he sensed a knowing, an awareness, of something wonderful taking place amidst the chaos. He was uneasy about the situation, but ready to face his destiny head on.

Chapter XXII: Skull Mountain

From where he was standing, the mountain seemed far away. He figured that if he was lucky, he could make it within a reasonable amount of time, if he pushed himself. There were trees and brush all the way to the mountain, but it didn't appear to be a thick jungle, like the planet surface was prone to be.

Zevon confidently got up and began to walk. He noticed he was more aware of what he was seeing, than usual. It was as if he were walking with someone else inside him, an inner counselor, pointing out possibilities to be considered and warning him to avoid walking in certain directions. Confidence grew in Zevon. He knew he was not alone and his heart and mind were one in the destiny that was awaiting him.

The mountain now loomed in front of him. It looked formidable with steep cliffs and, from where he stood, there didn't seem to be any easy passageway to the top. He decided to walk around the base of the mountain for a distance. Maybe he would see a path, or maybe a cave, that would lead him to the top.

The walk around the base proved futile. The mountain was just too wide and there were no visible accesses to the top that he could see anywhere. Then Zevon noticed that there were heavy vines hanging all the way down from the mouth of the skull. His heart told him this was the way to go. Slowly, he tested each vine to find the strongest one.

The mountain was not a large mountain, by Mauldronian standards. It may have been 3,000 feet high, but it was a sheer climb to the summit and he had to admit, a perfect fortress for Gar. Considering that it was all underground, Zevon thought the place to be quite remarkable.

Zevon had a sense that something could happen at any time. He decided not to look down as he climbed the vine. He was never too fond of heights, anyway. His mind couldn't escape wondering about what he was going to do once he reached the top. Something inside told him not to worry. When the situation became apparent, he would know what he had to do.

About 1,000 feet from the top, Zevon could see what looked like guards standing near the mouth of the skull. That must be the entrance, he thought.

Fortunately, he could see that the lip of the skull stood out far enough that they would not see him if he stayed quiet.

Zevon rested for awhile -- it was good that the vine was strong and large enough for him to do that. It was hard work and he was sweating heavily, both from the climb, and from the adrenaline pumping through his system. While he rested, he welcomed the cool breeze which helped him catch his breath and calm down.

The skull was not only a large fortress, it also appeared to be a castle. It was apparent to Zevon that this was Gar's home, not just a large cave. There were many window-like openings all over the summit that became visible the closer he climbed to the top. He found he was excited and anxious for whatever was going to happen next.

He slowly swung his body over the edge of the protruding edge that formed the skull's mouth. The guards were stoic and facing away from him. His heart pounded as he quickly slid to the side of the skull's mouth, into a crevasse that would give him cover.

He took a couple of minutes to catch his breath and then slowly peeked out to check on the guards. Again, they were stoically facing away from him. His mind began to argue with his courage. Could he make it into the actual entrance and not be caught?

Zevon's heart reminded him that he was okay and he must move forward. He took one more quick peek at the guards and then slowly tiptoed towards the mouth entrance. Sweat began to pour down his face. He had never realized that he could sweat like this, but he had never been tested like this before, either.
About five yards from the entrance, he stopped to calm himself. Then with a quick burst of energy he ran

as fast as he could the rest of the way to the entrance. His heart pounded as he turned the corner. With a loud thud, Zevon fell backwards. He had hit something hard and the collision blurred his vision. He closed his eyes for a moment.

When he opened his eyes, they had cleared and he gasped. Before him was the figure of a guard. He had run into a guard, but the he didn't move. The man didn't appear to be reacting to Zevon at all! Zevon slowly stood up. When he closely inspected the guard, he realized that it looked real, but it was only a statue. With a sense of relief, he turned around to see that the other guards were, too. He wanted to laugh, but the image of the slain Giron sobered him quickly.

Zevon had to admit, the fortress was beautiful. It was filled with crystals and beautiful furnishings that immediately sent Zevon's heart soaring. Creatures he had never seen before, in his world or this one, freely roamed the inside of the castle. They were peaceful and playful. He also noticed a hall directly across from him. His heart told him he must go into it.

Where was Gar? He was more perplexed than ever now. He wanted to let his guard down, but the thought of Anggar's body and the missing Diron haunted him. He walked to the other side of the entrance hall and looked around. There he could see that this entrance was only a small part of a large complex with numerous rooms.

Each room was beautiful and full of objects that Zevon had never seen before. Where in this castle was Gar holding the Diron captive? He walked about 100 yards further
down the great hall, when he came upon a stairway that climbed to a series of rooms upstairs. His heart told him to follow the steps to the next floor.

On the upper floor, Zevon found himself in a large bedroom that contained all manner of strange devices. There was an incredible view from a terrace that overlooked the entire castle's domain.

At the back of the room was a bed with long black linen draperies that would shield anyone who was in it. Zevon had to look, and slowly walked towards the bed. His heart pounded as he crept quietly near to see if there might be an opening in the draperies that would reveal someone, or something, hiding inside. He found no way to see inside and realized that he would have to open the draperies himself.

In one fluid motion, Zevon grabbed the draperies and yanked them wide open. To his amazement, he found Xela lying there, either asleep or unconscious. He stood there for a moment, stunned and frozen in place, wondering what to do. He had just decided to reach out to her when a loud voice from behind startled him.

"That will do no good, boy. She isn't asleep, but under a spell." said a familiar voice.

Zevon turned around abruptly and there in the middle of the room, he stood face-to-face with the dark being who had taunted him at the bridge.

"Who are you?" Zevon asked the menacing being.

"You mean you haven't guessed who I am, by now?" he replied, sarcastically. "This is much too easy. I was actually hoping for a greater challenge from you."

"You're Gar, aren't you?" Zevon asked.

"I am." replied the being.

"What have you done to her?" demanded Zevon.

"I have, so to speak, captured her soul and the souls of the Diron people you brought to me." boasted Gar. "You have done well -- for a fool, that is." Gar taunted.

"What are you going to do to us?" asked Zevon.

"Nothing!" exclaimed Gar, angrily.

Zevon was feeling very uneasy. He didn't trust Gar any further than he could throw him. "I don't believe you." Gar laughed a hideous laugh and then pulled off the hood that had covered his eyes and face. Zevon was repulsed, and Gar smiled as he saw the raw expression on Zevon's face. Zevon had never seen such a horrible looking being in his life. Not even Anggar had looked that horrible.

Gar's ugliness was not just physical, though. He had an air of deception and meanness about him that was pure evil. Gar was obviously overly obsessed with manipulating his victims in whatever way pleased him. Zevon thought, how odd it was that he would notice, and yet he realized that it was his heart revealing the creature's true nature and vile purpose.

"What is it that you want of me?" asked Zevon boldly.

"I have a special favor to ask of you." the creature answered, playing with him. "By the way, if you don't help me, then I will just kill them all."

Zevon was angry, but his heart reminded him to keep cool and, above all else, to observe and listen.

"You are going to find the Door of Ohah for me." Gar demanded. "My health does not permit me to go on such a strenuous journey." Zevon doubted that he was being told the truth. Gar spoke again. "I will start you on the path, but you must locate the Door at the entrance to Ohah and then you will come back here and take me there. Oh, and one more thing," Gar continued, "you have 24 hours of your time to find it or I will kill them. Do not test me, boy. I will do it."

Zevon believed him. It was probably the only thing Gar had been truthful about and Zevon felt that same chill again.

"First of all, Gar, you must show me the Diron people. I want to see for myself that they are alive and well." Zevon demanded.

Gar gritted his teeth and scowled at Zevon. "All right. Come with me." he replied angrily.

Zevon followed Gar down a long dark stairway into a large underground chamber. At first, Zevon had trouble adjusting his eyes to the dim light. When they reached the bottom, Zevon could see that the Diron were in a comatose state, much the same as Xela had been in upstairs in the bedroom. They were breathing, but other than that, they were motionless. Zevon instructed Gar to wake Zir, so he could speak to him.

Gar leaned down and touched Zir with his staff. Immediately, Zir took a deep breath and sat up. Zevon touched him gently on the shoulder so Zir would know he was safe. "Zir, are you all right?" he asked telepathically.

"Zevon, my friend, it is so good to feel you again! What has happened?" he asked tentatively.

"All of you are being held prisoner by Gar. He has put you under a sleeping spell, or something." Zevon confided.

"Enough!" Gar shouted. The shout immediately caused Zir to hold his ears and squeal in pain. Gar then touched Zir with his staff and he fell unconscious again. "You have seen that they are all right! Now go! Find the door for me or I will see to it that they never wake again." he sneered.

Zevon glared angrily at Gar, as he smiled back at Zevon with contempt literally bleeding out of his pores. "I will find the door for you, Gar, but if you harm the Diron in any way, I promise I will destroy you." Zevon warned.

"Destroy ME?" laughed Gar. "Boy, you are barely out of diapers, and hardly aware of your capabilities. I am 900 years old and I most assuredly know mine. You don't threaten me!" he shouted back, pointing his finger in Zevon's face. "Follow me and I will start you on your path in the right direction." Gar told him.

They walked back up the steps and then down the rest of the great hallway to a huge metal door. Gar handed Zevon a helmet made of an unusual material. He told Zevon to not take it off or he would lose communication with him. Gar also told him that the energies behind the door would blind him without the helmet.

"Now go. You only have 23 hours left to find the door or your friends will all die. Prepare yourself for the change in atmosphere." Gar told him as he opened the heavy door.

Zevon stood back as the metal door slowly swung open. The light was intense, but not burning. His heart immediately sensed the incredible flow of energy, but Zevon could not yet recall where he had experienced it before. He stepped outside and beheld a place like no other place he had ever seen before.

Chapter XXIII: The Land of Ohah

What he saw was nothing short of spectacular. Everything glowed with an energy that you could feel flowing throughout your whole body. Zevon had never felt so joyousl in his life. This was like something out of a dream!

Gold and crystal composed most of the place, but there were also groves of trees, lush grassy meadows and the most beautiful rolling hills stretching for miles and miles.

This place looked much like the land of Gar, but only in its structure. The feeling that enveloped him here was one of elation and a total sense of wellbeing. Something inside told him that it was safe to remove the helmet, and remembering Gar's warning, he removed it *very* slowly.

Gar had lied to him. There were no ill effects at all! He was glad it was off because now he could get a better view of this magnificent land. His heart told him that this magical and beautiful land would not allow any negative thinking about anything.

Zevon decided to follow the path that stretched before him. It was made up of the most beautiful blue quarry stone that he had ever seen. The path took him through thickly wooded areas and gradually climbed a slight hill. He noticed a light source and it seemed to be peeking over the hill at him and he naturally felt compelled in his heart to investigate further.

As he continued along the path, he marveled at how brilliantly colored everything was. All of the different hues were luminous and seemed to be full of life. It gave Zevon the unmistakable feeling that he and everything here was all connected somehow -- by what, he didn't know.

Zevon had to fight an overwhelming urge to get caught up in the exhilarating energy of this land. He had to keep reminding himself that he was there to find the Door of Ohah and then return to bring Gar to it for whatever reason he had. Only then, could he rescue the Diron people.

Zevon walked several hundred yards when a wispy flash of blinding light flew past him calling out his name. He stopped momentarily, and tried to see where it went, but it was gone. He walked further, maybe another hundred yards, when he saw a glowing object coming towards him. Standing perfectly still, before him appeared the most beautiful creature he had ever seen. It was glowing white, nearly transparent, and wearing a warm smile.

"Greetings, Zevon!" said the lovely creature.

"How do you know my name?" Zevon asked, amazed.

"I have been waiting for you and I've watched you ever since you arrived." The being told him . "My name is Ala, and I am the guardian of Ohah, the land you are in now. You have come seeking the door to the entrance of Ohah and Gar has captured your friends to use as a trade." The creature explained.

"We have known of Gar's plan for some time. Understand, Zevon, he cannot enter into this land because his heart is closed. Innocence and openness of the heart are required for those who walk here. Without it, they would perish. You see, Zevon, everything within this energy grows to its maximum potential very quickly. Love reveals itself here in waves of ever-increasing awareness. Evil can come in here, but it is soon seen for what it is, and all who harbor evil intent then perish within their own misguided perceptions."

"Gar was once like you, but in his desire for power and control, he thought manipulation was the way to greater awareness. His inner lack of respect and self-love caused him to use others as crutches. He was never able to get past the door. His disfigurement was caused by looking beyond the door, when he was warned not to. See, he was not ready. His inner ugliness and evil immediately manifested outwardly."

"Gar was once a handsome young man, but through the centuries, he has gotten worse within himself, and the outside always reflects the inner nature." Ala smiled, and told Zevon that the answer to his situation would be found in the Castle of Mirrors. "You will meet the old man there and he will help you rescue your friends and solve the mystery of your journey." With that, Ala quickly transformed into a ball of bright light and then was gone.

Chapter XXIV: The Castle of Mirrors

Zevon walked for several miles. The path then wound crookedly through an open field and up over a small hill. He had been thinking about the old man and why he had not met him sooner. He also wondered why he had to deal with Gar at all.

Upon reaching the top of the hill, Zevon saw still another breathtaking sight. It was a majestic castle made of pure crystal. It sparkled when light touched it and he had never seen anything so magestic. Although he was still over a mile away, he could feel the incredible amount of energy emanating from it. The path in front of Zevon now changed from the blue quarry stone to pure gold. He walked down a path lined with beautifully trimmed trees, topiaries, and the greenest grass imaginable.

About two hundred yards from the castle, he came upon his first obvious obstacle. There was a moat surrounding the castle and there didn't seem to be a way across to the castle.

Zevon shook his head in frustration. This was no usual moat either. It was at least a thousand feet down and, instead of water, it was roiling with molten gold. Zevon's mind stretched to come up with a plausible solution, but his heart was coaching him to relax and listen from his center within.

Zevon was sure he would need help to solve this dilemma, so right there in the middle of the path next to the golden moat, he sat down and began to go within to find his center. He found it easy to relax and go within here, near the energy of the land of Ohah. Soon Zevon found himself being greeted by all kinds of loving, smiling faces. He hoped to talk to some of them, but they whisked by as quickly as they had come into view. Zevon saw he was headed right for a growing speck of light in front of him.

"Greetings in light, Zevon. How are you?" asked the familiar voice as he slowly came to a stop.

"Hello there!" replied Zevon joyfully. "You are the Greeter that I've talked to before."

"That's right, and I'm here to assist you." The Greeter replied. "You are faced with a problem that all beings have difficulty with on their journey towards self-realization. The mind wants to calculate and analyze how to solve the problem and that only makes the solution harder to find. I'm going to give you the secret, Zevon, so just relax and pay attention. Reality is whatever you believe it to be. I'm not talking about in your mind, but in your heart. Most people try to solve the impossible in their minds, but it's the heart which houses the soul.

"Religious people make the mistake of thinking they have to find their soul with their mind. The soul can't be found with the mind. It must be felt with the heart. Life force is not an object the mind can hold. Life force is living, feeling energy that's unstoppable and ever-changing. It responds to your intent. The unconscious mind will tell you you can't do something, until the heart shows you how. The heart reveals that you are the creator of the obstacle. It's the *knowing* that makes miracles possible."

Zevon nodded. He understood what the Greeter was saying.

"Now, my friend, I want you to feel your soul and feel and imagine yourself on the other side of the moat. Do not think about it, just feel it in your heart, the desire of being on the other side." the Greeter told him.

Immediately, Zevon began to feel himself expanding. The Greeter had disappeared into a fog of light. Fear started to grip Zevon and for a moment, he perceived that he was totally out of control, but then a voice within assured him that he was okay. It told him not to think about what was happening, but to stay in touch with his feelings.

Zevon felt strange. In fact, he didn't feel like Zevon at all. He felt powerful and also compassionate. He had crossed some barrier of awareness and by looking within, he remembered that he had placed himself in this world with these restrictions. Zevon struggled with confusion. A loving inner voice, however, helped him keep his mental balance. From this place he knew that he could cross the moat and he knew how he would do it. There was no doubt, only certainty.

When Zevon awoke, he found himself in the same position he had started in, lying down on the path, relaxing. This time, however, he found that he was on the other side of the moat. He sat still for a while bathing in the energy and awareness of what he had just experienced. He realized for the first time that to seek power was useless, for he was power, itself.

As he walked the last 100 yards, he could feel and see that the castle was a powerful center of energy and awareness. It was like straddling the border between the world he had just come from and the world here in Ohah.

In front of the castle were seven golden steps that climbed through an open door at the top which exposed part of the inside of the castle. There were words on each of the seven steps, words which he could read. They were in some strangely written language but, in his awareness, he knew their meaning:

HUMILITY - COMMITMENT - SACRIFICE - AWARENESS - HONEST SELF-REFLECTION - GRATITUDE - SELF LOVE.

Zevon knew instinctively that these were the lessons that he came to Garbon to learn. He never dreamed that his suffering could have had such a perfect meaning. Now, it all made sense to him.

He walked up the stairs and into the inner hallway of the castle. Everything was fashioned out of crystal, gold and mirrors -- there were mirrors everywhere! He walked out into the middle of the hallway, hoping to see his reflection in the mirrors but, to his surprise, nothing appeared in the mirrors! He was puzzled and decided to investigate them more closely.

Walking to his left, he reached up to touch one of the mirrors and the hand of an old man came out of the mirror to touch his. He immediately jumped back.

Looking at the mirror from where he sat on the floor, he saw a familiar face from another past inner journey. It was the old man.

Chapter XXV: The Room of No Reflection

Zevon stepped back as he stood up. Before him and stepping out of the mirror was the old man, who before had helped him find the door. He looked regal, thought Zevon. He elegantly wore a long purple and violet robe. His hair was as white as snow. In his hand , he held a small crystal ball, which he held out in front of him and it seemed to radiate energy in tune with his movement.

The old man smiled at Zevon and then motioned for him to move to the center of the room again. Then he spoke ."This, my friend, is the room of no reflection. Do you know why it is called that, Zevon?" the old man asked.

"No sir. I do not." replied Zevon, respectfully.

"You don't have to be so formal, my friend. My name is Oman and I will be your final teacher on this journey. It is called the room of no reflection because it has mirrors that you cannot see your reflection in." he joked. Zevon gave him a puzzling glance. "Lighten up, Zevon. I am about to teach you a very powerful secret. When a being has discovered the power of their inner life force and doesn't get caught in outer illusions anymore, they realize they can control their destiny. It means that they stop giving their power away to outward circumstances. They realize, finally, that they are power themselves."

"You have no reflection because you are awakened to the fact that your personality is a vehicle your soul is using to teach you certain values in this life. Do you not feel very solid within?" he asked. "Are not my words jumping with life in your heart?"

"Yes!" responded Zevon joyfully. "I feel as if my awareness is everywhere. I feel that I am creation, itself. I understand you and I even understand myself better now. I know who I am and what I have come to do." The words rolled out of Zevon's lips before he fully realized what he was saying.

"You have no outer reflection because your energy has been raised to the point where you don't need outer verification of who you are. Rather than being trapped in your dream any longer, you can now consciously choose to create the one you want."

Oman let his words soak in and then continued. "So many people in other galaxies fail to see the simple truth that their outer world is a reflection of their beliefs. Sadly, their beliefs are not the totality of who they are. Do you understand, Zevon?" he asked.

"The difference is the mind and the heart then." said Zevon.

"Precisely!" exclaimed Oman. "The mind thinks and believes, but the heart feels and knows. Life is feeling. It is simple existence without analysis or criticism. When you live in your mind and ignore your heart, you cut off the very force of the inspiration and creativity that sustains your life. You become a prisoner to your thoughts and, often, the perceptions of others.

The reason you met Gar was because, deep within, you still have a belief in the duality of good and evil. You also don't trust in the deep nature of your power yet. YOU FEAR IT. You must Accept it, Trust in it, Believe in it, because it has only good intentions for you." Then

Oman concluded the conversation with a hug of deep affection.

Chapter XXVI: The Seven Steps

Oman told Zevon to follow him up a set of stairs and then they went out to the front of the castle. There, they could look out over the Land of Ohah. It was truly majestic and so beautiful. He smiled at Zevon and then pointed to the steps directly under their feet. "Do you remember these steps?" he asked.

Zevon nodded that he did. "Never forget the writing on them, my son. They are the steps to the Door of Ohah. Each is a key that unlocks the power of your heart." Oman explained.

"I've wanted to ask you about the Door of Ohah. Gar sent me here to find it for him. He is holding my friends hostage and will kill them if I don't return to The Land of Gar to bring him back here to the door." said Zevon."

"Yes, of this, I am aware. Rest assured, Zevon, you have already found the Door, but it's not at all the way you supposed it would be. The Door of Ohah is the door to your heart -- it is not a physical door at all. Most people make the mistake of thinking that, by some magic charm, fable, or by having good luck, they will change their destiny. The truth is, if they don't change their heart or, at the very least, better know their heart, they will remain always prisoners of their fears, doubts and ignorance. The mind and its thoughts can be horrible taskmasters." Oman told him. "It is time for you to leave, my friend. You have only three hours to get back, before Gar carries out his threat." said Oman.

They walked back to the stairs. Oman told Zevon about the nature of the castle. He said the mirrors were actually gateways to other dimensions and times. All of them were far more beautiful and infinitely more mysterious than even Ohah. Zevon was stunned. He told Oman that he wished he didn't have to go back. Oman gave Zevon a very serious glance and then told him, "I have a surprise for you, my friend. You do not have to go back, if you do not want to."

Zevon stared at Oman for a few minutes, as he let this new information sink in. Then his eyes widened in joy and excitement. "But what will happen to the others, if I do not go back?" he asked in wonder.

"Gar will indeed kill them. But, Zevon, remember, they have all chosen this path for their learning. You aren't responsible for their fate." Oman confided.

Zevon thought about this for a moment and his mind twisted in agony. He knew the Diron and Xela had done much for him on the journey and teaching him what he needed to know. He made up his mind and slowly shook his head as he said, "I'm sorry, but I must go back, Oman. They're my friends and their sacrifices have brought me here." Zevon told him proudly.

Zevon's eyes filled with tears as he looked at Oman. "Will I ever see you again and this place?" He asked.

Oman put his arms around Zevon, hugged him, and whispered, "NEVER FORGET THE POWER OF WHO YOU ARE."

They walked to the bottom of the steps and then Oman stopped. "I have something I want to give to you, Zevon." Then Oman reached into a brown leather bag studded with diamonds and sapphires. He brought out a small crystal ball which he handed to Zevon.

"Whenever you need to touch your inner wisdom, just hold this in your left hand and touch your heart with the right one." said Oman.

Zevon looked anxiously at Oman, and then he took the crystal ball as it was handed to him. "You will know how to deal with Gar, when the time comes. Do not fear! Your love within is greater than his greed. Besides, the door is in his heart, too, but he will have to choose whether to open it. Neither you, nor I, can do that for him." Oman explained, sadly.

Zevon walked down the seven steps and, as he turned to say a final goodbye to Oman, he saw that Oman had already gone. Zevon realized that he had to face what lay before him alone, relying on his own strength. He could not rely on anyone else.

He walked back down the hill and followed the path once more, hurrying to make it back in time to save his friends. He was so lost in thought about everything he had learned from Oman that he was startled when he suddenly found himself standing in front of the door at the back of Gar's castle. The door swung open and Gar waited for him just inside the entrance.

Chapter XXVII: The Light

"Well, boy, you cut that very close. You nearly didn't get back in time." Gar snarled, sounding a bit disappointed. "Did you find the Door?" he asked.

"Yes, Gar, I found the door, but I'm afraid I cannot take you to it." Zevon said, nervously.

"What do you mean, you CANNOT take me to it? Of course you can! You mean you WON'T take me to it! " Gar angrily shouted.

Zevon realized that there was no way he could argue the issue about the door with Gar. Gar would never understand or believe him.

"I have made a shield that will allow me to go into the light safely. You will guide me." insisted Gar.

"Listen a moment, Gar. A door does not exist." Zevon explained, slowly making each word distinct. It isn't a *physical* door, Gar."

Gar's heart was closed to Zevon, as well as his ears to any explanation, and he became furious and began to throw things around the large room. "I told you to find me the door and then take me there, or I would kill them all, didn't I? " he shouted. "I'm also going to kill YOU!" he screamed, racing towards Zevon.

In one reflex move, Zevon calmly and instinctively reached into his pocket for the crystal ball, just as Gar was nearly upon him.

Gar stopped in his tracks. "No, No! Put it back!" The ball glowed brilliantly in Zevon's outstretched hand. "Where did you get that?" Gar yelled, covering his eyes.

"Oman gave it to me." replied Zevon.

Gar screamed in anger and pain. "I never told you to contact Oman! I told you to locate the door and come back to lead me to it!" shouted Gar angrily. "What did that crazy sorcerer tell you anyway?"

Zevon put the crystal ball back in his pocket and explained slowly, like speaking to a child.

"Oman told me about you, Gar, and he taught me about the Door of Ohah. He helped me to find it within myself because, like I told you, the door is not a physical door. It's a door that is open to those whose hearts are innocent and humble."

"Don't preach at me, boy." scowled Gar "I've been on this planet for nearly 900 years and I know more about power then you can even begin to imagine. I can control and create whatever situation I want tothat fits my whims." snickered Gar.

"That's not entirely true." said Zevon, as he pulled out the crystal ball again.

Gar immediately covered his face with his cape. He begged Zevon to put it back. Zevon promised he would, but only after Gar had taken the spell off of Xela and the Diron and everyone was released.

Gar paused and then said he would, but Zevon must not bring out the crystal again. Zevon told him he would keep it hidden, but only if Gar released the hostages. Gar held his staff out and touched Xela lightly on the shoulder while she was resting on the bed. Slowly she yawned as she woke from her deep sleep, and then her eyes opened.

"Zevon!" she said, smiling. Then she saw Gar. "Why did you do this to me? I never meant you any harm."

Gar didn't say a word. He only glared in contempt at the innocent girl. Behind Gar, Zevon could see the very top of Zir's head as he came up the stairs. Zir told Zevon the remainder of the Diron were standing hand in hand downstairs in the great hall, where they would be waiting. Gar had apparently sent one of his creatures to guide them from the cellar.

"What do you intend to do now, boy?" Gar asked.

"We're returning to the Land of Ohah. I'll be taking Xela and the Diron with me." he replied.

"And me?" Gar asked, petulantly, like a spoiled child.

Zevon shook his head, expecting this. "You will be left here, but I do have a surprise for you, Gar."

Gar glared in outrage as the Diron passed by him in the great hall. He desperately wanted to do something, anything, to stop their escape, but he was afraid because Zevon held a Soul stone from the Land of Ohah. It was obvious to Gar that Zevon was not aware of the stone's purpose. Gar knew that the Soul Stone magnified the energy and intent of the person who carried it. If Zevon were to become angry, he could easily destroy Gar.

The last of the Diron had finally passed by Zevon and Xela. Then Zevon handed the Soul stone to Xela and walked to the front of the line so he could open the door to the land of Ohah. Brilliant light peeked through the cracks from the other side of the door. As Zevon opened the door, he told Zir he was free to walk through the doorway and feel his way into the kingdom. "I have one last thing to do and then I will be back to assist all of you." Zevon told him, as he returned to Xela's side.

"You have done well, Zevon. I'm very proud of you." Xela told him with a smile. "You'll love the Land of Ohah and we'll have such fun together."

Zevon smiled back at her. "I want you to go with the

Diron and make sure they all get into the Door. "I have something I must give to Gar, before I go. I will follow when I am finished."

She handed him the crystal and walked down the tunnel, encouraging the Diron to keep moving along.

Zevon told Gar he could remove the cape from his face. "I mean you no harm, Gar, but the time for your games is over. You and your kind always seek to control and imprison those who are weak, ignorant, or less fortunate than you. You use fear and manipulation to force others to do your bidding. You treat them with disrespect, because they don't respect themselves. Their misguided imaginations look to people like you for guidance, when the only guidance they truly need is to listen to their hearts. You, too, are not without hope, if you will only take the time to listen to the faint whispers of your heart." ended Zevon.

"Do NOT lecture ME, boy." scowled Gar.

"Then I have nothing more to say." Zevon answered, sadly. He knew he could do nothing to help, if Gar was unwilling to help himself.

"What was that about a surprise that you said you had for me?" Gar asked, pouting.

Zevon smiled and said, "Here catch!" and he tossed the crystal at Gar's feet. It surprised Zevon to see that the ball did not glow. Gar, being curious, reached down to pick it up, forgetting about Zevon's exit.

Gar screamed just as Zevon was opening the door to the Land of Ohah. He knew that Gar's lust for power and greed would cause him to pick up the Soul stone. What Gar had forgotten was that the stone amplified the energy and intentions of the one holding it. Gar immediately was reduced to particles of dust and atoms. His soul would be sent to a place where the loving guidance of the universe would re- educate him and allow him another chance to listen to his heart.

Chapter XXVIII: The Decision

Zevon caught up with Xela at the front of the line. They were both going to lead the people of Diron to the Castle of Mirrors. Suddenly, Zir spoke up and excitedly told him they no longer needed Zevon and Xela to guide them. Zevon was surprised and asked him why.

"Because we can see you, Zevon! We can see Xela, too, and everything all around this beautiful land!" cried Zir. "I don't know how, but this energy, the wonderful magic that's here, is allowing us to see you and the land in our mind's eye. It's as if we had real eyes!"

Slowly, one by one, the other Diron people cried out in wonder and excitement. They reported that they, too, were seeing for the first time. Great joy erupted among them, as all the Diron pointed at what they had never seen before and each other. Telepathically, it was a mishmash of 6,000 elated voices all talking at once.

Zevon and Xela walked hand in hand down the path to the castle. Xela told Zevon of all the wonders he would experience and all the dimensions that they could travel to through the castle's mirrors. Xela was truly happy for both of them.

"Wait. Something isn't right, Xela." Zevon felt alarmed, but didn't understand why. "I should be happy, but I'm not."

"What's wrong, Zevon?" she asked.

"I don't know, but I think your grandfather will tell me when we arrive at the castle." Zevon told her. They spent the rest of the journey enjoying the scenery and each other's company. Zevon was troubled, though. He had always believed that once he found the Door and was with Xela, he would be at peace and happy. Not even the high energy of Ohah could pull him out of this unexplained sadness that was gripping him.

When they finally arrived at the Castle of Mirrors, Oman was standing on the outer steps smiling. Xela rushed to give him a hug. Then she proudly told her grandfather about how Zevon had rescued them from Gar. Oman gave Xela a huge hug in return and then slowly looked over at Zevon.

"Do not be alarmed at your sadness, Zevon. It is normal, considering the destiny that awaits you." Oman explained.

"I don't understand. Have I done something wrong? Zevon asked him, concerned because of the way he was feeling.

"No, no, not at all, my son. You did fine. Close your eyes for a moment and tell me what you see." requested Oman.

Zevon did as he was instructed and his mind suddenly focused on Mauldron. He had almost forgotten about Mauldron! He felt a deep sorrow as he thought about his former home. He began to see pictures of home in his mind. Something terrible had happened, or was about to happen to the planet!

"There has been a revolution on Mauldron since you left, Zevon." Oman gently told him, jolting Zevon from his inner calm." The people of your planet have overthrown the Council and smashed the main computer system. They refuse to live like machines any more. The pain you've been feeling is your soul's connection to those people, because of the common destiny you share." He finished.

"I have to go back." Zevon said, concerned about the welfare of his family. The words surprised him as they came from a place of knowing deep inside his heart. He looked at Oman and Xela. Both were smiling, because they knew what his reaction would be.

"We knew that you could not stay Zevon. We've known it all along. You had to find the truth out for yourself." said Xela as she walked back over to his side.

"You mean that all this has been a game, a plot, to get me to go back?" Zevon asked, incredulously, with hurt visible in his eyes.

Xela put her hands on either side of Zevon's face. "Listen to me, Zevon." Tears were now flowing freely down her cheeks. "Your soul chose for you to have these experiences, so you would remember the teacher that you are. Your heart was asleep and, had it not been for all of this, you wouldn't be aware of your destiny or the powerful being you are."

Oman broke in." Zevon, you came here to honor your heart and to discover the unlimited potential of your being. Now your heart is calling for to you to decide if you will stay or, perhaps, go back to teach others what you have learned. Like so much of what you have learned since you came here, we cannot decide for you. No matter what you decide, please know there is no right or wrong decision."

Zevon admitted that it would be wonderful to travel to other dimensions, but confessed that his heart would never be at rest if he didn't at least try to help his people. After much thought, Zevon answered,

"When can I go back?"

"The shuttle will be arriving this day. We will both escort you back to the surface of the planet, if that is what you wish to do." Oman promised.

Zevon smiled then and hugged both Xela and Oman. Together they walked down the hill to a cave that would take them to the planet's surface again. Along the way, Zevon met Zir and told him goodbye.

"I will miss you, my friend, but the bond that you feel with your people is the same kind of bond that caused me to also lead my people." Zir told him.

Zevon turned to Oman and asked him, "What am I to teach my people? I don't know where to begin, or what I should say."

"Trust your heart, Zevon. Your heart will reveal to you all that you need to know. You won't have to seek them out, because one by one, they will find you, a few here and a few there. You will know them because their heart will be like your heart." Oman told him. With that, Oman handed Zevon a very old parchment that was tied with a blue ribbon. He told him to not open it until he was in the shuttle on his way to Mauldron. Oman told him there were special instructions inside that he would need to follow.

One last time, Zevon hugged his friends and told them goodbye as he walked up the path through the tunnel. Soon he found himself back on the planet's surface. In fact, the tunnel's entrance was hidden on the surface by the wrecks and machine parts that he had passed through when he first arrived!

Zevon thought about Anggar as he walked past the wrecks towards the landing area where he had been left by the shuttle from Mauldron. So much had changed since then and it seemed like a lifetime ago. He thought about all of the beings and experiences he had here on Garbon and how they each, in their own way, taught him and helped him to see.

Zevon's thoughts were broken by the sound of shuttle engines roaring in the overhead sky. He was glad to be going back to Mauldron, even though he would miss Xela terribly. But he was comforted by the fact that they shared the same feelings, and he knew he would see her again. He now trusted his heart and listened to what it told him. He had learned so much here on Garbon and his life was forever changed. He would see her again, because he knew he had the power to go wherever his heart desired to be.

Chapter XXIX: The Letter

Zevon couldn't see the shuttle operator, but the hydraulic door opened as he walked up the ramp and into the ship. This was one of the larger shuttles. Unlike the smaller ones, this had two sections, one for cargo and the other housed the control room for pilot and passengers. Once he was inside, the hydraulic ramp and door automatically closed.

Zevon waited patiently for the pilot to open the door to the control cabin. Once it began to open, Zevon stepped inside and there sat every member of his family! They were smiling at him, and his mother was the shuttle pilot.

They were so happy to see each other and they cried and hugged each other tightly. Zevon asked his parents what happened on Mauldron. His father explained that a great revolution had occurred and the people were confused about what to do. The computers had always made their decisions for them and now they would have to trust themselves. He said in spite of the overwhelming fear and anxiety, the people would not go back.

Zevon sat down as the ship lifted up and left his temporary home on Garbon, the place where he had learned so much. His mind returned to Xela and Oman, and he smiled, feeling a warm glow. Then he remembered the parchment and letter that Oman had given him. He untied the blue ribbon and read the letter:

> *My Dear Zevon,*
>
> *You have a lot of work ahead of you. Many will not understand you. There will be some who think you're out of your mind and they will seek to persecute you.*
>
> *It is useless to persuade people against their will. For this reason, I am cautioning you against preaching what you have learned. It is not up to you to save their souls, but for them to discover and use their own inner power and light.*
>
> *For this reason, I have given you a very old parchment, which I received when the higher forces of the universe placed me in my position. It contains The Seven Steps of True Power. Read it when your heart is full and have copies of it made into books for your people. Those whose hearts are ready will understand it and seek you out.*
>
> *Help them to understand, without interfering, and those who are ready we will bring to Garbon. It is the desire of the universe to heal your planet and you are a part of that plan.*

Love and Light,
Oman

Zevon put the letter next to him on the seat, so he could read the parchment. No sooner had he laid it down, than the letter began to glow and then the glowing disappeared before his very eyes. Zevon grinned as he thought of Oman and the Land of Ohah. Magic wasn't dead and the heart is not a liar!

Then he opened the seal that held the parchment.

Chapter XXX: The 7 Steps of True Power

As Zevon unrolled the old parchment, it crackled under his touch. Excitement filled his heart as he wondered what it would reveal. He adjusted his position in the seat for comfort and began to read.

"To those longing to escape the shackles of their mind and learn the freedom of their heart, we, the beings of light and love, offer you these principles:"

There was a space of about an inch down the parchment and then the writing continued.

"Power, to most of you, is an external and objective thing. In your future to come, however, power will be more subtle and far more subjective.

Fear is the motivation for power, as you have experienced it. Separate from the soul, the ego (mind), fearing for its existence, ever strives to control and manipulate to its advantage. The ego does not realize it has created this and it can just as easily create from love or faith.

Choice is at the heart of power. You have not chosen power, because you were born into an energy field that supports a belief in the lack of power.

The grand illusion of your lives is that you think you are powerless and alone when, in fact, you have all the power you need to create the life you want. You must decide that you deserve it and claim it back.

The path of power is your heart. That which you love and dream to be is, in essence, your soul's desire for you. Follow it and you will release your soul, your true identity, and your power.

The universe is not run by haphazard rules that serve no purpose. It is not a joke or a mistake that you forgot your power, because the heart of power requires that you realize one important key to your journey back

to yourself. The key is that you must love in order to give your soul's love in service to humanity.

Power is not given by the universe to control and manipulate people. That power comes from men fearful of being taken advantage of by their fellow man. True power comes from deep inside the soul and serves to enlighten and heal all it touches. There is no need to manipulate or

control, because ego fear is replaced by the love of your soul.

Truth is the expression of your soul's love on the earth plane. therefore, truth is subjective and personal. Your truth is not another's truth. Therefore, your power may not manifest like another's. Your purpose and the purpose of another is not the same.

You are coming to a time when individual self-expression will take a turn for the better. As your people turn their ego's in for the power of their soul's direction, they will begin to reclaim their power and create their own life and realize it is okay to be themselves.

The heart of power is guided by seven principles of true power which define and monitor its expression. Each without the other is useless, but together, they form a chain that balances the expression of power with its source of inception.

First Principle: Humility

Be aware that we need to turn to something greater within from time to time to solve the problems of life. Sometimes, we realize we're afraid and troubled and in need of help beyond our normal conscious awareness. We have the desire to serve the universe with our own unique gifts under the guidance of spiritual forces, knowing that each person in our life reflects the beliefs we hold subconsciously within. They are the mirrors of our soul and we owe them our love and forgiveness.

Second Principle: Commitment (To Yourself)

If you don't know and love yourself, you'll never create your own reality. To love yourself is to love the soul you are and to express your life through that soul. You must let go of the crutches in your life and surrender to the depths of your soul. We all have only one lover that is true, immortal and infinite; it's the soul. All other lovers are only reflections of levels of growth to be attained and transcended. I'm not saying you shouldn't have lovers, but put them into true perspective and love your soul. It will love you back.

Third Principle: Sacrifice

Sacrifice the rational and intellectual mind for the

knowledge of the soul. The soul sees without time. It knows, without space. To sacrifice the mind to the soul is to be in step with the universe. We are all part of the universal mind, but the ego (mind) cannot sense that greatness -- only the heart, alone, can believe. When we place our mind, our rational life, into the hands of the heart, something wonderful happens. We stop struggling and, when we do, we see why we're where we are and can then hear how to get out of the dilemma. Knowledge is power, but not rational knowledge. True power comes from your heart.

Fourth Principle: Awareness

Awareness is the heart's ability to work WITH the universe, not against it. You may have a great idea and lots of money, but without awareness of what the universe wants, you will fail miserably. Awareness comes from surrendering to the ultimate guidance of the heart.

Fifth Principle: Honest Reflection.

If your life is working, then you are in sync with the universe. If your life isn't working, then you aren't in sync with the universe. Many live less than satisfying lives because they lie to themselves about their career, marital status, and lifestyle. Fear guides them and a general distrust of themselves causes suffering because they don't take total responsibility for their lives. When you fear to know yourself, you create illusions to live by which all pass with time.

True power is knowing who you are and being who you are without judgment. It's a connection to your heart and soul which allows the higher purpose of your life to manifest in your life, causing healing. Healing is the right use of power. When you can live and forgive, then you will heal and your power will be restored in totality. Until you love your life and open your heart to forgive all that has offended you, you won't know the peace, power and the marvelous miracle of love that you are.

Sixth Principle: Gratitude

Each thing that happens in your life is a reflection of the beliefs you carry within. Each crisis shows where you're using your power against yourself. Gratitude is the cure for self-pity and a healing balm for depression. Gratitude opens the heart.

Seventh Principle: Self Love

You are the creator of your life and your future. It's up to you to love yourself where you are and to love your dreams into existence. You cannot be forced to do that. The Universe merely waits on the fringes of your reality to welcome you home.

IT'S TIME TO COME HOME. PLEASE COME HOME.

The Ghost of Woodstock

The Ghost of Woodstock

It was the summer of 1989 that I will remember for the rest of my life.   I was seventeen years old and aspiring to become a great rock musician.   I had already been in several bands and studied music for going on ten years.

That particular summer, I had made plans to go to a camp for aspiring rock musicians in upstate New York. The best part was, the camp was run by musicians who had had some success in the business. Their specialty was guitar and, at the time, I thought I was really bad.

My name is Mike and this is a story that I had to tell. I know many people will not believe me, but for those who do, I know it will change their life.   It has more than changed mine.

The camp was at a place called Woodstock, New York. I had heard about it over the years, but since I didn't live during the 60's, it meant very little to me. Hippies just seemed stupid to me and that whole time period was like a visit to a foreign planet. My musical history was like the whole Vietnam War in many ways. A large show of force with little success.

I guess I had, or still have, a pretty large ego, but I will never forget someone I met at music camp and the lessons he taught all of us.

He told me that I was not allowed to say his name. He said it would not be necessary, because those reading this story would know who he is. I thought it was all kind of weird, but who was I to argue? I mean it was *him* after all.

He told me that I had a message to deliver for him to all the young people who love rock music. I don't think I would have the courage or strength to write this if it wasn't for the fact that he gave it to me to write. Even now, I find it hard not to say who he is, but you'll have to forgive me. I gave my word.

CHAPTER 1: SUMMER OF 1990

I remember it was hot, humid and downright miserable that summer in New York City. I was fortunate to have been born into a well-to-do upper middle class family, so we did have air conditioning.

Both of my parents are working professionals and I don't recall ever seeing both of them together for even a month. I suppose it's not all their fault. They travel a lot, you see, and their various responsibilities keep them at work late.

Music has been my one salvation since I was in junior high. I don't know why, but I love it and I want to express myself through it. What I can't express to my parents openly, I can say in a song or on my guitar. I guess you know by now that I'm pretty lonely. Well, at least I was.

I have no brothers or sisters and my friends are few. The friends I do have are also musicians. We understand each other and seem to have a lot in common. The one problem I share with my friends, though, is that we all have big egos. I've never met a guitar player who is serious and who doesn't have an ego.

At times it's helpful, but I've been in some pretty bad fights because of it. The other problem we have is that drugs and heavy metal music tend to go hand in hand. I am no angel, but I know my limits. He helped me to see those limits. I'm talking again about the guy whose name I can't tell you. I respect him because he knows where I come from.

I think it was June when I saw the ad in the Times for serious rock guitarists. I had just finished my junior year in high school and I was determined not to spend the summer in the city. Don't get me wrong, the city is great, but for some reason, that year, I just wanted to get away.

I was concerned about how my parents would react when I told them I wasn't going to college. It was hard to explain, but I knew I wouldn't learn what I needed to know in college. I was a gypsy at heart and I always found people to be a source of the best education you could have.

At that time, I also began to realize I needed to get away from some bad influences, you know, friends that were not as serious about life as I was. I looked at this musical camp as a challenge and, to be honest, I wanted to find out if I was as good as other guitarists from all over the country.

Anyway, I told my dad about the camp and he and mom were glad to give me the car and money to go. It would give them two weeks of freedom from me in August. I need you to know that I don't hate them. I sometimes wonder what they're for. It seems we only tolerate each other for the most part.

The summer of 1990 went too slow for me. I spent most of it hanging with my musician friends. We jammed a little here and there where we could. My nights were spent writing music and playing my guitar.

I have a girlfriend, but the time we spend together isn't as important to me as my music is. I don't think we'll be together much longer. We both know the end is near. My trip to the camp and meeting him have caused me to see my life differently now. I know that I don't need to cling to others for my emotional security.

I remember August that summer as being really strange. I should have known the camp would be bizarre in some way, too. My friends and I were fighting and my girlfriend got pregnant by another guy in a different band. What a life, I thought .

Finally the day came for me to leave for Woodstock. I was so glad to be leaving the city. My parents and I said a very brief goodbye and then I was gone. The freedom I felt was good as I left the city and drove north. Luckily the weather wasn't too humid and I could drive with my windows down.

I had to laugh as I thought how my parents would react if they saw what was in my suitcase. I packed two pairs of jeans, underwear and three torn t-shirts. Period. You have to understand, I needed room for my records and music. You were only allowed to bring one large suitcase and your guitar with an amp - - yes, I also brought along some grass.

The trip to Woodstock was uneventful, except for the state trooper that pulled me over. What a jerk. I don't think he had any real reason for stopping me, other than to hassle me. He gave me some lame excuse and looked the car over real good. I admit, I was concerned he might make me open the trunk and look in my suitcase. Would my parents crap ...

The place where I was going was an old country retreat between Shokan and Boiceville. Woodstock was right nearby. The camp was on a plot of land that included a pool, riding stables, and gardens. At the time, it sounded like a monastery to me, but for the sake of the music, I decided I would give it a try.

After several hours driving, I finally reached my destination, only to get lost. I asked a gas station attendant for the directions to Tavor Hollow Road. He told me to go here and then turn there and he nearly drove me out of my mind. I decided to smile and just thank him.

Finally after two more hours of driving, I came to the road I was looking for. I made a right turn and started down a long dirt road. It was like being out in the boonies. The estates out there were separated by acres and acres of land. New York City born and raised, I never saw that much space between houses.

At last, I came to the end of the paved road and it turned into a gravel driveway. About a mile down the driveway, in the middle of some trees, was this large old house. It was in great shape, well kept, but not at all like the houses I was used to seeing in the city.

Those were mostly old brownstones that were butted up against each other so close you could borrow a cup of sugar without ever leaving home.

As I got closer to the house, I could see a lot of cars and several people unloading them. I decided it was time to put on my cool attitude -- had to protect my vulnerability and keep people at a distance. My image was at stake.

I pulled into the parking lot in front of the pool and was immediately greeted by this goofy looking dude. "Hey man, welcome to camp. My name's Earl." He said.

I looked at him, smiled, and walked to my trunk to get my stuff. He asked me if he could help me unload the car. I thanked him and told him I could get it.

The house was larger than I thought. It had about eight rooms and seemed very comfortable. I'd never kept my own room as clean as this. From what I could tell about the other people there, the owners were risking severe damage if we partied.

My first shock was on entering the registration area and finding out that we had girls at the camp. I wanted to say something smart, but decided not to cause waves this soon. The guys at the registration desk were older dudes. I'd say they were at least in their forties. My first thought was, how are these guys going to show me anything? They probably haven't touched a guitar in twenty years.

Next we went through the usual roll call and I paid them the rest of my tuition. They told me to go back out through the door and turn left, then go down the steps to the basement. I put my guitar on my shoulder and picked up the amp and suitcase.

Walking towards the stairs I could hear people talking and laughing. The stairway was a real pain. I had to turn sideways to go down the narrow stairs. I was hoping to get to the bottom without incident, but I guess it wasn't my lucky day. My suitcase and amp were banging the walls on either side, and I couldn't see my feet too well so I misplaced my left foot on the last step.

It was a great entrance. I fell into the room to the approving claps of several people I didn't know. How embarrassing.

As I started to pick myself up, a girl came over and asked if she could help. I tersely told her I was okay while I glared at the people around the basement.

Within a few seconds it was like I didn't even make a grand entrance. They all went back to talking and telling stories in their little groups. I found a place in the left corner of the basement for my stuff and I sat down. Then I counted the chairs on the floor and deduced that twenty-six people were in the camp.

The girl who tried to help me up came over and introduced herself. Told me her name was Gina. I acted cool -- I didn't want her to know I thought she was cute. She told me to relax and not worry, nobody was going to bite me. I smiled and lit up a cigarette.

We talked for a while and she gave me this piercing look and said I had a real attitude. With that said, she promptly left my company.

One of the older guys came down to the basement and asked us to take our seats.

"All right dudes and dudettes, listen up. I'm Speed, your instructor. I'll be in charge of the sessions this week. My purpose right now is to tell you about camp. If you have any questions, please wait till I get done talking and I will answer them."

He told us there were rules we had to observe while at camp. One was, we were not to leave camp and go to the nearby towns. Another was, we weren't to leave our sleeping quarters after curfew. The biggest bummer was that we weren't staying in the house.

Apparently, there was a campsite on the property with a meeting room and several cabins around it. He said we'd have plenty of time to jam on our own and that brought rousing applause from all of us.

I was beginning to have my doubts about this camp. There was this stifling energy about it that annoyed me. I was hungry to meet someone who could speak my language, someone I could talk to. The problem was, I was too shy and defensive to even ask. I wanted them to come to me.

I looked around the room at the other people. What a crew. They were from all over: Los Angeles, Miami, Detroit, even Denver. I tried to feel them all out to see if anybody had good vibes.

Then somebody punched me in the shoulder. It was her, Gina. I asked what her problem was. She told me I was her problem. I wasn't used to girls being that direct. In New York, we have plenty of mouthy ones, but this one had my number and I didn't know if I wanted to be pinned against the wall.

I felt she knew the me that was hiding inside and she wanted to expose him. I told her I thought she was pushy. She just looked disgusted and told me to have it my way. I tried to ignore her, but each time I peeked out the corner of my eye, she was staring at me. Finally, I gave in and asked her if she wanted a smoke. She smiled back and said sure. I definitely wasn't comfortable being that vulnerable, but I just felt that I needed to connect with someone.

We talked for awhile and then I was jolted when the whole room stood up at once. I was so caught up in our conversation that I hadn't listened to the directions the instructor was giving.

This girl was beginning to get to me. I felt really comfortable with her. We not only had a musical interest, but I felt we shared a personal interest, as well. I told myself that I didn't want a romance. I came to camp to discover more about myself musically. This was definitely going to be interesting ...

When we were dismissed, we picked up our gear and headed back up the stairs. I asked a guy next to me what we were doing and he told me we're going on a two-mile hike to the campsite. I sighed, made a face, and looked over at Gina. I really didn't want to lug this gear too much further.

The sun was shining as we walked outside. It was good to get some fresh air. The smoke in the room was really beginning to get to all of us.

Out behind the main house, there was a barn and a horse trail that snaked along beside it and then took off up over a hill. Our instructor told us we were to follow this path to the campsite. I marveled at what a pretty place this really was. The path even took us through a working orchard.

We walked about a mile, when I asked an instructor how much farther we actually had to go. He told me we would be there in about 15 minutes. I asked him if I could stop for a minute so I could move my stuff to the other shoulder. He smiled and said I could rest for a minute, but they would continue on up the hill to the camp down the other side. He said I couldn't miss the camp, if I stayed on the trail.

It had been a while since I had done any hiking. I wasn't in the best shape and my smoking didn't help my breathing any. I set down my luggage and amp and sat on them to smoke a cigarette. The group reached the top of the hill and I saw Gina turn to smile and wave, so I smiled back and waved her on.

I was just starting to feel stronger, when out of the corner of my eye, I thought I saw something move. As I turned and looked in that direction, I saw a red blur move behind a tree over in the orchard. It made me feel real uneasy. I yelled toward the tree and asked who was there. I sort of thought maybe one of the guys in the group was pulling a fast one on me. There was no answer. A cold chill ran up my spine as I took a long drag on my cigarette.

I didn't like being alone in a strange place and the feeling of being watched made me feel anxious. I put my guitar over the other shoulder and picked up the amp and suitcase. As I took a couple of steps towards the hill, a voice (or actually more like a whispered voice) seemed to come out of a gust of wind that blew past me. I heard, "Hey man. What's your hurry?"

I'll tell you honestly, goose bumps popped out all over me and another chill ran up my spine. I didn't look back even once as I picked up the pace of my walk. I sure don't remember any scenery that was around me on my way up that hill, either. I was too scared to look around.

When I finally reached the group, I was drenched in sweat. Gina took one look at me and asked if I was okay. I said I was and went about my business. There was no way I was sharing what I may (or may not) have seen with her -- or with anyone else for that matter.

The campsite was something else. There was a small lake right in the middle and scattered throughout the woods were numerous cabins. Off to the left of the main path was the mess hall. It was all kind of cute and the camp was well-situated on several acres with tall pines and various leafed trees.

The group was told to walk up the steps to the mess hall and wait inside until cabin assignments were made. I was glad to be able to sit down, dump my equipment and rest again. I also welcomed the opportunity to stop sweating.

I just couldn't stop thinking about what I had experienced back on the trail. I wanted, needed, to tell someone, but I was afraid I might be called a kook. Besides, I didn't really know WHAT I had experienced back there, anyway.

Gina came over and asked how I was. I told her I was just tired. She gave me this queer look and told me that I wasn't telling her everything. Her insight made me angry and I snapped at her to mind her own business. She gave me a look like she wanted to punch me in the face. Instead, she just called me a jerk and walked away. I guess I deserved it.

The head instructor finally came back and started handing out our cabin assignments. There would be five people to a cabin. The one exception to the rule would be the cabin assigned to the three girls that came to camp.

I was beginning to feel a little guilty about the way I treated Gina, but I was too proud and way too uncertain of what to tell her. I mean, I really hadn't seen much of anything. How do you describe a whispering voice in the wind?

At last, I was assigned to my cabin. It was the one highest on the hill that cradled the whole campsite. I think I told you, I'm not crazy about being alone in a new place, but the idea of spending two weeks with total strangers was even less thrilling.

The cabin was an experience in primitive living. Each

cabin was probably about twelve by fourteen feet square, or something close to that. We each had a cot and a school-type locker right beside it for our stuff. There was one window facing the lake, and a card table to eat or play cards on. The front of the cabins all had a porch where we could hang out.

One by one, we all left the mess hall after dinner and headed to our cabins. When I got close to my cabin I could sort of guess who my roommates would be. Up to this time, I had not made an effort to meet any of the guys -- of course none of them ran right over to greet me either.

It's a funny thing about pop rockers. They can be friendly, but they do like to size each other up first. It can be a real head game, but their sensitive perception to energy causes them to feel out people and situations. We definitely live on a different wave channel than everyone else.

I walked into my cabin just ahead of the other guys. As the rest of them walked in, I nodded to them, but we did not immediately talk. As I said, I had a way of feeling people out first. It was a way to prepare myself for a friendly encounter and to protect myself from an unpleasant one.

As I mentioned earlier, rockers all seem to have big egos. They liked to strut their stuff, but they're real defensive about people getting too close, or at least that was my perception of the ones I had known before coming here. In actuality, I think that was how I always felt about myself.

The first guy to come in was a short Mexican dude. He had a friendly face, but I could tell that he was undisciplined. He seemed young and unsure of himself. It also appeared that drugs were a normal part of his lifestyle. There were old needle tracks on his arms.

The second guy that came in looked real menacing. He had an angry energy about him. I told myself I bet he was good, musically, but he probably had trouble getting along with others. I knew I would have to be diplomatic with this one, or all hell would break loose. He had all kinds of tattoos on his body and I wanted to laugh, but I wasn't in the mood for a fight.

The next guy to come in the room was the most interesting. I hadn't seen him before, but he seemed strangely different from the rest. When the instructor came in behind him, I suspected that the reason why he seemed different was forthcoming. He told all of us that the guy was blind and we would have to help him at times. We all smiled and glanced knowingly at each other. Nobody wanted to be a nurse, but we knew we had no choice.

The last guy to walk in was the cream of the crop. Anyone could tell he was wealthy and a real snow job. There was an obvious phoniness about him. I also thought to myself that this guy was not to be trusted. Watch your stuff, I cautioned myself.

A silence came over the room as we all settled down and studied each other. The Mexican dude was so nervous that he pulled out a Playboy magazine and started to read. My menacing friend glared at each of us as he fooled with his guitar. But the ice finally began to break when the wealthy dude asked if anyone wanted to play cards.

Of course, my enthusiasm suddenly wilted away when he talked about playing for money. I didn't like the idea. He seemed too slick and sure of himself and I felt he had something up his proverbial sleeve.

All of us told him we didn't have much extra money. Our menacing black roommate said he had none to spare at all. Finally, it was decided that we would play just to kill some time. One other problem we had was that one of us was blind.

What a crew. I helped the blind guy to the card table. There we were, five strangers who didn't even know each other's names yet. I decided to risk it and introduced myself, so I put my hand out to shake the menacing dude's hand and told him my name was Mike. He promptly slapped my palm and said his name was Percy. Everyone else followed suit. It was good to open things up like that. Somehow everything seemed friendlier in the cabin after that.

Surprisingly, the card game turned out to be fun. We all opened up in subtle ways and a feeling of trust began to emerge that wasn't present before. I actually found myself laughing at myself for prejudging these guys so unfairly. It taught me a lesson and my little protective world didn't feel so lonely anymore.

Right when we were having the best time, a voice came booming over the PA system. It politely informed us that dinner would be served over at the mess hall in thirty minutes and we should prepare for it. We all groaned our disapproval, but had to admit, we were hungry.

Each cabin had one small bathroom and shower in it. We decided to shower in shifts and the others lay on their cots for a short nap. I thought again about the experience on the trail. I had a feeling that something weird was going to happen at this camp. Fear blended with a stubborn curiosity as I wondered what it would be.
I guided the blind guy to the path that ran by the front of our cabin and the five of us walked together to the

mess hall. On the walk, he said his name was Billy Johnson, and he'd been blind since birth, but he wasn't the type to ask for pity or special treatment. I found I was both respectful and curious about Billy. I don't know why, but I felt that he, even more than myself, was very musically in tune.

The mess hall was buzzing with activity. It appeared that we weren't the only cabin where its inhabitants had broken down the barriers to each other. I didn't realize that twenty-eight people could all act so rowdy. The three girls were the worst.

After dinner, we all got a surprise. The head dude came in and announced that each of us was to stand up and tell everyone the reasons why we came to camp. A knot swiftly developed in my stomach. I was not adept at, or keen on, speech-making and my personal reasons for coming to camp were ... well, mine.

One by one, each person in the group got up to tell his or her story. Some had no special reason for being there. Others admitted wanting to get away from home or the city. I was surprised that the guys in my cabin seemed more intense than the rest. We were all searching for something. What we actually sought was elusive, but we were definitely hungry for something.

Finally it was my turn. Not knowing yet what I was going to say, I slowly pushed my chair back, stood, and began with my name and personal history in music. Then something strange came over me. I had planned to be quick and pointed, but my feelings got in the way. A calm came over me and everyone else who was there. I told them I came to camp to find the true heart of my music.

The only way I can describe it was that I felt a part of me reaching out and touching everyone else. Even Gina had a soft smile on her face. Without knowing the rest of the individuals in the group I realized that we had all somehow connected that night. We were all looking for exactly the same thing -- until now, we just didn't know what to call it, how to find it, or even where to look for it.

The walk back to the cabin that night was a quiet one for me. I had touched something inside myself that night and now I wondered if I would ever feel it again. Several of the group members came up to me to shake my hand and pat me on the back.

Gina even came up and hugged me. It caught me off-guard and I asked her what it was for. She smiled and said I should consider it a medal for being myself for the first time. I protested, but she held her fingers up to my mouth and told me not to ruin a good thing.

Inside, I was restless and confused. My mind wouldn't shut itself off and, besides, I didn't want to sleep anyway. We couldn't play our instruments until morning, so I tossed and turned in my cot watching a full moon blast its light through our only window. Suddenly, I got this idea to take a walk, but we weren't allowed to leave the campgrounds, so at first, I just went out on the porch and stood staring into the night sky.

CHAPTER II: The Walk

Damn the rules. I walked around outside and looked up the hill that our cabin was snuggled up against. The path we walked to the camp went straight up to the top. A light of some kind flickered at the top of the hill and I decided I had to check it out.

The hill wasn't steep, but the lighting was terrible and I tripped over some tree roots which were above ground. Once I got to the top of the hill, I was surprised to see that the flickering light was a campfire off in the distance, about fifty yards away. I couldn't tell if there was anyone around. The brush between me and the fire was blocking my view.

All sorts of weird thoughts came to me as I stood and watched the campfire. Would some bum come out of the woods with a knife? Could one of the instructors have camped out to look for people like me who were breaking the rules? I knew they warned us not to leave the cabins at night and if I got caught, I knew I would be sent home. Yet, for some strange reason, I really didn't care. I felt the camp couldn't give me what I was looking for anyway. The instructors were cool and the group had touched me that night, but I was burning inside with a passion to share my music. I just didn't know how to do it.

Slowly, I walked closer to the fire. Several times I cringed when I stepped on dry branches that cracked loudly in the otherwise silent night. Daniel Boone I was not. I felt stupid sneaking up on the site. Odd, the fire seemed to glow brighter the closer I got to it. There was nobody around. The fire was situated within a perfect six foot circle. The burning wood snapped and popped as I surveyed the location. It was almost as though it was waiting for someone or something.

Then a chill went down my spine again -- man that was becoming a common occurrence around here. There was a tree on the far side of the fire and something, or someone, was over there leaning against it. From that distance, I couldn't tell who or what it was. The glare of the fire and the shadows playing across the scene obstructed my view.

I skirted the fire and, to my further surprise, I realized that it was a guitar leaning up against the tree. It was an old model. A Fender Stratocaster. It was pure white and looked to me like it had taken quite a beating over a lot of years. I wondered who could have left it there. Where were they now? I decided to sit down by the fire and play some with the guitar. It had a wonderful feel to it and a strange joy came over me as I coaxed out its mellow notes. I didn't know why I felt so happy -- maybe I secretly hoped no one would come back to claim it and I could keep it.

"You dig my ole lady, man?" came a voice out of the dark.

I jumped and my heart dropped right into my stomach as I quickly put his guitar down and stood up. "Sorry, I didn't see you." I said nervously.

"That's okay. She likes you." he said.

I was confused by the conversation, especially the words coming from the strange black man standing in front of me. He looked different, like someone frozen in time. I remember I wasn't afraid of him, but he did look oddly familiar.

"Should I know you?" I asked.

"Nah!" he snarled, as he sat down.

He sat straight across from me on the other side of the fire. At first, I was apprehensive and didn't know quite what to say. His face had an underlying sense of sadness about it, but there was also a charm and grace about him. I liked him, but man, I sure wondered who the dude was.
"You can call me James Marshall, if you like." he said out of the blue. I started to tell him my name and he

stopped me by saying he already knew my name. he said I was Mike.

I began to feel very defensive at that point, but he smiled at me like an enchanting magician and told me not to worry. I was in no danger and time would reveal to me the answers to all the questions in my mind.

He asked me how I felt and I told him I felt great. It wasn't a lie -- in fact, I couldn't recall ever feeling so good. It was so weird. Just being there, I had a sense of a greater awareness about everything. My mind even raced with new insights about my music.

I asked him where he came from. As an answer, he pointed first to the stars up above lighting the night sky, and then slowly, he pointed to my heart. Weird. I just looked at him and laughed. He didn't respond. Then he motioned for me to hand him his guitar.

I handed him the antique pure white Stratocaster that had seen much better days. He smiled at me again with that same ornery grin, as though reading my mind, and then he closed his eyes and began to play.

I couldn't believe my ears. I thought I must be dreaming. The tremendous sound quality coming from his guitar was the same as if it had been hooked up to several huge amps. I quickly looked around to see where the extra sound could be coming from, but everything looked normal. There was no way to explain the phenomenon. It was like ... well, like magic.

He stopped for a minute. "You all right, man?"

"Yes sir!" I spoke. "I only noticed that your guitar has no amps connected to it and yet the sound is so, well, so loud. We'll wake up the entire camp!"

"Can't happen." he said.

"Why not?" I asked.

"Because this night and this meeting are for you and no one else, Mike. The sounds and the sights you are experiencing are merely illusions that are built from your own desire to learn." he said.

My heart began to burn inside me. I understood him. He was right. Something incredible and yet strangely magical was happening to me here in his presence. I couldn't explain it, but inside I knew this was exactly what I was hoping I would find here at the camp.

"Didn't mean to scare you on the path up here earlier, by the way." he said.

"So, you're the one I thought I saw and heard on the path!" I exclaimed.

"Good for you!" he said, as a smile started in the corner of his mouth and then lit up his entire face.

"I'm here to help you find the soul of your music, Mike, you and any of the others that desire to find it." he said.

"You're a ... a ghost, aren't you, James?" I suddenly asked as I finally gathered my courage. A chill crept up and down my back, yet again.

I knew what I was asking was true, and the experience sent the cold reality racing to my mind. This man was dead.

"Don't let that ghost crap fool you." he said. "I don't haunt people. We spirits assist people who really want to know the truth about themselves. So, I will assist you in your search for understanding, but I cannot make your choices for you."

A sense of wonder flooded through me. I asked him to disappear right in front of me.

"Mike, I'm not here to play games and entertain you. If what you've seen so far doesn't convince you, then you don't want to believe ... or have to come back, either." he said sternly.

"Wait. Look, I'm sorry. It's just that his is all so, well, so incredible to me. I'm okay, really, but what the hell do we do next?" I asked him, still trying to take all of it in.

"Easy, man. You and I are going to share our little secret with the others who came to camp. I only want to see the campers. I don't want to see the instructors." he said.

"Why is that?" I asked.

"Because the instructors think they know it all. Their hearts are closed to the magic of music. They can teach technique, but the freshness, the inspiration, the ultimate magic of the music is not in them anymore. They've believed in others, but they've failed to believe in themselves." he sighed.

"The first law of your music, Mike, is that it's yours and no one else's. My music was mine and yours will always be yours." he said. "Don't ever make the mistake of believing anyone can teach you music. Notes can be taught, yeah, but the music has to come from the heart. You teach yourself the music."

I looked at him thoughtfully, while his words echoed in my mind. Then he handed me an album cover.

"You are to play this album every night of camp for the two weeks you are here. Tell those who come to you that you got it from the man who lives on the land next to camp. Tell them nothing more. Bring those who ask to meet me to this spot every night at midnight. You'll have to be sneaky, but all of you seem to like breaking the rules anyway." he laughed.

I looked at the cover but it was blank. He smiled and told me not to worry. He said the music was a composition that he had been working on for twenty years. "Just play the music," he said. "They will come."

"The second law of music, Mike. Trust what you feel and forget the critics -- that means your own analytical mind as well as all the professionals." he said. "Music is an infinite river of light, color, and sound. It cannot be harnessed, classified or categorized. It just IS and the true musician knows and respects that. He lives to embrace it daily."

A marked quiet came over me. I was so touched by his words, I could have cried. I had never spoken to anyone who could so eloquently express exactly how I felt about music. After a long pause, he nodded to me and said, "Our time is up for now."

"When will we get a chance to talk again?" I asked him.

"You and I will meet one more time, on the last night of camp." he answered.

I started to protest, but he told me it was important that I leave after bringing each of the others to meet him. I turned back to the fire to face him again, but he had gone.

That same coldness came over me again. I had the album in my hand, his message in my head, and the path back to camp out in front of me. There was nothing more I could do but go back down the hill to my cabin.

As I walked down the path, the morning sun had already begun to creep over the hills in the east. I thought to myself, I had this feeling like I would be dead that day.

I walked into the cabin just as the sun began to shine through our window. The other guys were up and getting themselves ready for the day. Carlos, the Mexican dude, asked where I'd been. I told him that I couldn't sleep so I had gone for a walk.

"All night, man?" he asked.

I had the uncomfortable feeling he was trying to nail me down. "Well, I did get some sleep sitting under a tree." I lied. "This cabin is too damned hot to sleep in!"

"To each his own, dude." he blurted out.

That morning at breakfast, we got the first taste of what camp would be like. James was right. These guys were not progressive rockers. They wanted to talk technique, but we were all more interested in the metaphysical side of music, you know, how to bring it up from our heart.

I asked the instructor if we would be getting some practice time. He told us that we had the whole evening to practice, but our days belonged to the camp -- our days would be used to learn new guitar techniques.

Whatever aspirations I had for camp and these guys died with his words that morning. I would've gone home right then, but the experience of the previous night gave me some hope for being there. I knew something wonderful was going to happen at midnight.

The classes were informative that day, but boring. We spent most of the time clowning around and our instructor became exasperated more than once. The fact that the chemistry between me and Gina was heating up didn't help much. She was gentle and very sensitive.

At one point she played for the class. We could tell she was deeply in touch with her feelings. The music she played was her own and so beautiful. I never would have thought that a hard looking girl like that could be so sensitive and feeling. Her music blew me away.

By the middle of the afternoon session, I was suffering from my lack of sleep -- I dozed off. Finally, to the thrill of the class, I managed to fall off my chair and onto the floor. At that point, I requested to be allowed to leave class. The instructor wasn't happy, but he wanted to teach his thing and I was in the way. He agreed to let me leave class.

I went back to the cabin and my cot and spent some quality time in Z- land. The next thing I remember is waking up and seeing Percy staring at the album that James had given me. He told me I had missed a great dinner.

"Oh well. I needed the sleep more." I told him.

"What you got on here, man?" he asked. "I don't really know. A fellow I met recently gave it to me. It's his stuff. He said he'd been working on it for twenty years."
"Let's play it!" Percy said, like it was the greatest idea he'd ever had.

"Play it? On what?" I asked.

"Billy brought a portable turntable." he informed me. "We can play the record on that."

When Billy came in, we asked him if we could use his turntable and he said, "Sure." I decided to just let things flow at this point. Besides, I was curious about the record myself and, admittedly, I still had some lingering doubts about the other night.

I recognized James' voice immediately -- it came on first. He talked in that funny lingo of his. There was also that same mystical soothing quality to his voice. He warned the player of the record that they would never be the same after listening to it. He also dared the listener to discover the heart of his own music.

Percy stopped the record and asked me where I had gotten it. I told him again that a guy I met handed it to me. And, just as James instructed me, I told Percy the guy lives on the land next to camp. He just shook his head and said that the record was "weird". What he didn't say was that he heard a compulsiveness in the voice and his curiosity was raised about what was to follow.

The music on the record was exceptionally clear. It was a powerful guitar solo. I had never heard such passionate and sensitive music played on a guitar. The other two guys came over to sit down and listen, too.

We were all magnetized, literally mesmerized, by the music. It struck a chord within each of us and touched us deeply. I had favorite guitarists and music that touched my life over the years, but this music was not just hypnotic in nature, it was also healing in a strange way.

I looked over at Billy. Tears flowed freely down his face as the record played. Carlos and Percy sat there stunned and silent. I wanted to cry like Billy, but my pride got in the way. Besides, I heard James play and I felt the magic then, so this record didn't shock me quite as much as it did the others in the cabin.

Silence filled the room as the record finished, and the arm lifted and moved back to its resting place. I looked at the others and they were all looking at me. Almost in unison they asked me, "Where did you get this music?"

I hesitated for a minute and then I told them again that a guy I never met before gave it to me. He lived on the land next to camp.

"Mike, you're not telling us everything. Don't play games with us. We're your friends." Billy said.

I looked at the guys and just shook my head. Then that same voice came to me again -- the one I heard on the way up the path the first day here. It said, "Play the music and they will come." I almost laughed out loud. I was feeling like an unwilling Pied Piper.

Slowly the words came out of my mouth. "You guys are not going to believe this."

I told the three of them about the other night and what had happened. I did not tell them his name or what he looked like. Somehow, I instinctively knew I should keep some things to myself.

When I finished, Billy the blind dude immediately asked to be taken to him. The rest of the guys excitedly jumped on the band wagon, too. I told them they would have to wait their turn, because I was only allowed to take two at a time.

I hadn't told them that he was a ghost. It was hard enough talking about the old fashioned way he dressed. Percy, the black dude, said he sounded like someone out of the 60's. Percy was older than the rest of us and he seemed more familiar with that era. I told them I didn't know much about that. I was barely ten years-old at the time, and just discovering what music was.

I really wanted to stop the questioning, so I reminded them that the first two were to be taken to see the dude in about four hours. I also suggested that to be fair, we should draw cards to see who goes first. The two highest cards drawn would go first. Billy and Carlos won the draw. Percy was disappointed, but said he could wait.

"You guys know, don't you, that in the 60's, one of the most famous rock concerts of all time was held near here in Woodstock." he said.

We all looked at him with curiosity. Since the rest of us were around seventeen and he was twenty-three, he told us about the concert and the incredible number of people that attended. He talked about it with such reverence that the concert seemed to come alive to us as we listened.

I asked him how come he knew so much about the concert. He proudly told us that when he was little, his mother had gone to the concert and taken him along. The smile on his face told us that he had been deeply and forever impressed by that one-of-a-kind event.

"I knew, even at that age, that music would be my life." He said with raw emotion glowing in his eyes. "I can still see that dude playing the guitar with his teeth.

He was fantastic. I was only three, but I will never forget it. It's one of the reason's I came to camp. I wanted to be near Woodstock again."

"Who was the guy?" Carlos asked him.

"I don't remember his name. Mom was married to a Cuban guy at the time. He got deported so we went with him and lived in Cuba until about three years ago. When he died, she and I came back to the states." he said.

Billy threw out some names of guitarists that I had never heard of. He talked about this one black dude almost reverently. Billy told us that this guy, more than most other guitarists, was the one musician who was credited for the development of rock guitar.

I told him that it didn't mean much to me. I was very aware of modern guitarists of my time. They had influenced me greatly, but the earlier guys didn't really interest me.

"We need to get some sleep, Carlos and Billy. I was up till dawn the other night." I told them.

Percy shut off our only light as I was setting the alarm for 11:30 p.m. In the dark room, Carlos and Billy started to ask me more questions and I pleaded with them to go to sleep. I assured them they wouldn't be disappointed.

I jumped up as the noise from my alarm woke me from a deep sleep. I hadn't had much sleep the last two days and part of me didn't want to go. Billy spoke to me in the darkness. "I'm awake, Mike. You don't have to get me up. I didn't sleep at all, I couldn't."
I told him, "yeah, okay." My mind felt like it was under water. I wanted to get up and move, but my body was exhausted and moving only slo-mo.

"Michael, come on, we have to get up!" Carlos said as he grabbed my arm and tugged.

"Alright, Alright. Get back and let me up," I said begrudgingly.

Carlos and Billy were already standing near the cabin door while I got dressed. I asked them to sit down and be patient -- we had plenty of time and, besides, we were close enough to get there in ten minutes. There was no freaking reason to hurry.

Billy was particularly excited about going, but I could tell that Carlos was less enthused. I asked him what was wrong.

"I don't like this. It's spooky." he said.

I told him it would be alright. Another part of me inside was thinking, is he going to get a surprise! I hoped with Billy going along he would feel more at ease. Then Billy reached over to grab Carlos' hand. "It will be okay, my friend. I feel that we're about to have a remarkable experience. I need you to help me. Remember, I can't see." Billy told him.

Carlos smiled then. He and Billy had already become good friends. There was a new bond there that gave them both strength.

I remember there was a full moon that night. We walked out onto the front porch and I stretched to help the blood flow in my body. I was still somewhat groggy. Then we stepped off the porch and turned the corner of the cabin to climb the hill. Carlos helped

Billy along and I slowly walked in front of them to assist, if necessary.

We reached the top of the hill in about five minutes. I

was comforted to see the familiar flicker of light bobbing and the shadows bouncing off the trees. Closer still, and I could see the fire burning just ahead. Then I spotted the figure of James with his back to us as he faced the fire. He was playing his guitar.
The closer we got to him, the louder the music sounded. It was eerie, but also extremely soothing. It sounded like he was making love to someone or something.

James didn't move as we approached the fire. With his back to us, he began to speak in Spanish to Carlos. Carlos seemed pleased, because he had this goofy smile on his face. I gathered that he told Carlos to take Billy and sit across from the fire, facing him, since that's what Carlos did. I watched Carlos' face as he moved around the fire. His smile turned into a look of pure astonishment. At that point, James again spoke in Spanish and Carlos' smile returned.

"Mike, my man. It's time for you to leave. We have some work to do." James said.

"Okay," I told him, "I just wanted to make sure they would be alright."

"They'll be fine. I'll see to that." he answered.

I turned to walk back down the hill to the cabin and James spoke to me once again. "Mike! Thanks!"

"For what?" I asked

"For believing." he said

Now it was my turn to smile, and he smiled back. I admit, I did have some strong reservations about all of it. I didn't want to leave the others alone, at first. But there was something in his eyes that eased my concern. I could only interpret it as love and compassion. It was then that I realized, he needed us just as much as we needed him. A sense of joy filled me as I reached the crest of the hill.

When I got back to the cabin, Percy was up. Sitting there in the darkness, he nearly scared me to death. He asked how things were and I told him everything was fine. Immediately I went to my bed and crashed.

CHAPTER III: The Next Day - Day Two

I woke up that next morning to the sound of a bird singing. My back was to the window, so I rolled over to see where it was coming from. I couldn't help but smile, and tears welled up when I saw Billy. He was asleep on the floor in the corner of the room with his guitar cradled in his arms. The open window was next to him. The bird had apparently flown in and it was sitting on the neck of Billy's guitar.

The morning sunlight streamed through some cracked glass in one of the opened window's panes and a rainbow of colors covered the entire length of Billy's body. I saw it as a sign. I couldn't explain it, even to myself, but inside I knew -- Billy was different because of last night.

Carlos was still asleep in his cot. He, too, had his arms wrapped around his guitar. A pleasant smile covered his face -- no, a peaceful smile. Yes, that was a better word for it. I have to admit that I was envious for that one moment. Then I suddenly realized that I hadn't seen Carlos smile much -- not since he came to camp.

I was happy for him. He told us that he came from the East Side of Los Angeles. There, it was either music or the gangs, so he worked for two years to save up the money to come to camp.

Slowly, we all began to wake and get up. Funny, nobody said anything. Billy and Carlos could only smile, and Billy's smile touched me deeply.

When we first met, he told us he'd been blind since birth. His parents were not going to let him come to camp, so he ran away. I thought about the trust and courage it took for him to do that. Billy was already way ahead of us in many ways.

The black dude, Percy, was the last to wake up and he growled out a greeting to us. But even then, no one said a word.

"Well s'cuse me till I kiss the sky! You guys haven't become prejudiced, have you?" he asked.

"No." said Billy shyly." We can't talk about last night. It was too personal."

I could see that Percy was going to make an issue of this, so I decided it was up to me to diffuse things. Somehow I realized that, like me, Percy was afraid, afraid of being left out, maybe. I think we didn't really believe we deserved to make it. We both carried a grudge about life.

I walked over to him and put my hand on his shoulder. "Hey, man. Don't take it so personal. You'll get your turn." I told him.

He scowled at me and brushed my hand away. I hadn't seen that much anger in anyone's eyes in a long time.

"Look, whitie," he blurted out, "don't tell me not to take it personal. You three have already been there. It's easy for you to be so pleasant."

I was stunned. He rolled over in his bed facing away from me. I started to get up and then something inside made me stop. I put my hand on his shoulder again. "Percy, I know you're angry. I'm sorry if you think we're stopping you or hiding something. We care about you. We just need you to respect our privacy. Billy and Carlos need time to think about last night." I said.

Suddenly, Billy and Carlos came over to the other side of the bed facing Percy. Carlos spoke first. "Amigo, I'm sorry if my lack of speaking has caused you pain, but I cannot speak about last night. It must be felt -- here," he said, pointing to his heart. "You'll see. It will be special for you, too."

Billy interrupted. "Percy." he said, grabbing hold of his hand. "I want you to know that we care about you. I know that may sound corny, since we've only known each other a short time, but it's true. We do."

Percy hid his face, but we could hear a quiet sob. I could also feel the sincerity coming from both Billy and Carlos and I was moved by it and yet strangely jealous at the same time.

We each got up and left Percy to his privacy. We could say or do no more. Percy would have to make up his own mind.

Breakfast that morning was a rather somber affair. You could tell that the majority of those at camp were not happy with the agenda. That is, with the exception of Billy and Carlos. They looked and acted like two kids let loose in a candy store.

The last one to come into the mess hall was Percy. I felt sorry for him. He just got his food tray and went over in a corner by himself to eat. I think we must have embarrassed him, but I'm not sure.

The classes that morning were full of the same old stuff we already knew. Most of it I learned years ago. It was getting so bad in there, that we started throwing spitballs at each other out of boredom.

Finally it came time to play our music. Each morning we got a break and we were supposed to practice. Billy and Carlos played something together that I had never heard before. It was so good that everyone stopped and listened -- even the instructor. The song was joyful and uplifting. Whatever boredom we had suffered through the morning was gone when we heard that song.

Chapter IV: Gina's Turn

Gina left her seat and moved over next to me as Billy and Carlos stopped playing. She had the same mesmerized look on her face that the rest of us wore.

"What happened to those two?" she asked.

"I guess they found something." I said with a touch of sad regret.

"Well they sure didn't get it in this camp." she said.

I laughed because I was thinking to myself -- if she only knew! Then the thought came to me to let Gina hear the record. "Gina, can you come over to our cabin tonight after dinner?"

"Sure hot stuff. Whatchu got in mind?" she comically fired back at me.

I admired her directness, but inside, I was disappointed that she assumed I was making a move on her. "I have something I would like you to listen to. It's a recording and I want your opinion on it." I told her.

The expression on her face changed from orneriness to one of interest with just a touch of appreciation.

"I would be happy to, Mike. I didn't think you knew me well enough to value my opinion that much." she said.

I was feeling a little uncomfortable now. I was experiencing a feeling that I had learned to avoid in the past. Sincerity made me feel vulnerable -- I always felt I had to hide my fears and insecurity from others. "I value your opinion very much, Gina." I said with a smile, almost falling out of my seat from my honest reply.

She smiled back at me with an endearing grin and then, to my embarrassment, reached over to hug and plant a kiss on me.

I was too shy to say anything, but I was not going to spoil the moment. Something wonderful was happening to me in this camp -- to all of us, actually. We were opening ourselves up to each other and sharing the music we all hid inside. That music was the magic, a valuable part of the uniqueness which made up each of us.

We had some time off that afternoon, so I went back to the cabin, laid on my cot and listened to the record James gave me. It was eerie, almost ghostly in character. I had never heard anything like it, certainly not on any CD's I'd heard. Several other campers stopped by and asked about the music. They said they could hear it coming through the open window.

Where did I get it and who was playing the guitar?   I instinctively knew it was not their time to know yet. I brushed them off, but told them I would tell them about it later in the week. James had been right when he told me to "play the record and they would come ..."

Despite the fact that the record was heavy on electric guitar, it had a soothing, almost spiritual feel to it. It was like listening to classical music played on an electric guitar. It reminded me of watching eagles climb to high altitudes and swoop down on creatures for food. Such it is with freedom of expression and depth of passion, I thought to myself.

I had to admit, I was getting a little impatient waiting my turn. I had become unhappy with my growth and development on the guitar during the last year and I knew that something had to change. I felt I needed to find *something*, but didn't know what that something might be, or where to find it.

Just then, Percy came into the cabin. His mood had improved dramatically and he was deeply moved by the changes in our other two roommates. Almost instantly, I looked at him and knew that he would be one of the campers to go tonight.

When I told him as much, he immediately came over and hugged me. I mean, he gave me this huge hug! "Sorry, Mike, about my attitude. I've lived in the ghetto all my life and liking white people has not been easy for me. I had a younger brother who was shot and killed by a white cop some years ago. I guess I've never gotten over that." he said.

"I had no way of knowing, Percy. I'm so sorry to hear that happened." I said.

Percy looked away, but I could still tell that something else was troubling him. He looked like he wanted to talk more, but the tears in his eyes embarrassed him.

"What's wrong, Percy? I feel you aren't saying all that you wanted to say. You're holding back." I told him.

"I don't want to talk about it, but I need to, 'cause it eats me up at night." he said.

"I'll be glad to listen, if you want to talk about it." I told him in all honesty.

"Mike, you can't tell anyone. It's bad, man. I did something really bad a few years ago, something really awful." he whispered.

"I promise to keep it secret." I said, wondering what in the hell I was setting myself up for.

After checking to see if anyone was around and finding no one, Percy sat on his cot which was next to mine. He started to speak a couple of times, but each time, he choked on his tears and had to stop to compose himself. I felt so awkward in this situation. I wasn't used to signs of sympathy, but I knew pain -- and I felt he needed to know I cared. Instinctively, I moved to the cot he was on and put my arm across his shoulders.

"I killed a man, Mike," he said. Then he broke down, sobbing quietly as he stared at the floor and looked at me pathetically. He had been so tough-looking when we first met. Now he seemed so broken and very human to me. I felt for him.

"I decided to get even after my brother was killed. I hated white people and the pain wouldn't go away. I drank myself sick and used drugs to build up my courage -- see, I was too scared to do it sober, so I got high one night." he confessed.

At this point he stopped talking and it seemed almost

like the whole world was waiting for him. I could feel the pain he felt as he admitted to both of us what he had done.

He continued, "I saw this white cop go into a music shop. He parked his cruiser and went in through the side door in the alley. I was coming down the same alley, but he didn't see me. I was high and I had a gun. I hid behind a dumpster and waited." he said.

Percy looked at me like a child who was caught being naughty by a parent and wanted forgiveness. I told him it was okay, and to go on.

"When he came back out the side door, I shot him three times. I thought I would feel better getting revenge, but I didn't. I walked up to him to see if he was dead -- I was gonna finish him off. Mike, there was blood everywhere and he was alive and he was looking up at me! Christ! I had the gun pointed right at him and damn, I froze.

I tell ya, he looked at me like no guy ever looked at me before, and get this -- he told me that he forgave me! Shit, Mike, I panicked and I questioned my actions. What in the hell had I just done?

Then the last thing the cop did -- you're not gonna believe this -- he handed me this guitar. Geez oh fuckin' Christ, he didn't go for his gun or nothing like that. He just looked at me real sad and told me he wouldn't need the guitar now, but maybe I could use it someday. It was so weird. Then he died. I can still see that look on his face -- I'll always see the look on his face." Percy said, from under a batch of fresh tears.

"That was five years ago, Mike. They've never caught me, but that night hasn't ever left me, not for even a minute. For that reason, music became important to me ever since that night." he said.

I smiled at him then, feeling a warmth flood over me. It was rare that I ever had a chance to comfort anyone. Hell, I hardly knew how to comfort myself, sometimes, but I could feel the words inside that wanted to come out and I spoke them.

"Percy, I understand. I've done some things in my life that I've hated myself for, but my music was always able to pull me out of it. That cop gave you a gift that night. He forgave you, and he was the only one who had the right to judge you, but he didn't. He gave you your life back when he forgave you and handed you his guitar. Deep inside, you know it's now a part of you, and your life, but you have to forgive yourself, too, Percy." I said.

A new calm came over Percy's face. He understood what I was saying to him. I wondered for a moment if it was really me talking. I knew I had times in music when I felt inspired and was able to write or sing my feelings, but this was different. It was the first time I had felt compassion for another human being and spoke that way.

We both understood that in some way what he had done must serve a purpose. Nothing else mattered, except that he continue to explore the gift he had been given -- the guitar. It was then that I understood the power of forgiveness for the first time. I knew I would never be the same -- not since he shared that event with me. I began to search within for all the things I had not forgiven myself for.

After dinner that night, Gina walked back to our cabin with Percy and me. He was so different now. He smiled and talked to us like he had just won the lottery.

He was excited and the burden and anger he had carried for so long was now gone. I marveled at his transformation and I even envied him a little.

Gina sat down on the cot across from me, while I put the record on. Percy looked at her with a wild gleam in his eyes and told her she was not going to believe her ears.

I decided to play the back side of the record this time. I had been so engrossed with the first side that I hadn't listened to the back yet.

It started with the sound of the ocean and seagulls squawking. It made me think of a place I knew once in California where the ocean waves pounded the rocks and seagulls floated on the air currents.

Just as we all kicked back to relax and listen, the sweetest sound of a guitar began playing in the background. I could picture the sun on the skyline sinking into the ocean on a hot summer night. It was like a crazy salutation to the sun, like a thank you, for the gift of light that day. Gina's eyes were full of tears. Percy and I sat in a state of peace and calm.

"Where did you get this music?" Gina asked quietly.

"I can't tell you," I said with uneasiness, "other than to say I got it from a dude who lives on the land beside the camp, up on the hill."

"What do you mean, you can't tell me?" she replied. "I mean, I can take you, but I can't tell you where I got the music." I explained.

I felt like a fool. I didn't like playing games with Gina, but I had to keep my word to James. She looked at me in disgust, got up, and headed for the door.

"Wait!" I shouted, as I reached out to grab her arm. "You'll just have to trust me, Gina. I have someone I want you to meet, but I promised him I wouldn't reveal his name." I told her with humble sincerity. "The truth is, I don't know who he really is, but he gave me this record and told me to bring pairs of students up the hill every night at midnight to meet with him for the two weeks we're here." I said in total frustration.

Gina just stared at me and, for a moment anyway, I thought she was convinced. Then she began to laugh and between loud guffaws, she demanded that I stop joking with her. That made me angry but luckily, I caught myself and sat back down on the cot.

At that point, Percy came to my rescue. "Gina, he's not joking. I can't tell you any more than he already has, but I'm going tonight. Please go with me. I don't know what's up on that hill, but something tells me inside that it's right and I need to check it out." he said.

Gina was touched by the change in Percy and she knew his words came from a humble heart. "I don't know what's going on here, but if it's that important to you, I'll go." she said, looking at Percy.

I felt betrayed and hurt to think Gina didn't believe I was telling her the truth. I was stuck with all this anger and frustration boiling inside me.

"When do we go?" she asked.

I took a deep breath to take my mind off my feelings and told her we would go when it was dark and the moon had risen.

We all sat or laid quietly listening to James' music. I don't remember exactly what happened after that. I fell asleep. When I woke up it, was pitch black out and Percy and Gina were gone.

At first, I was frustrated that I'd failed to escort them. Then I felt angry that they didn't wake me. I had a sudden impulse to run up the hill and catch up to them, but my pride was hurt and I decided to stay in bed and chuck it all. Oh I'd get even -- no more escorting for me! I was through playing this game on his terms!

That next morning, I was slowly aroused from a deep sleep by a gentle embrace and two soft hands caressing my forehead. As my sleepy vision began to clear, I could see Gina standing there with this look about her. I could tell she understood my secret and I was happy for her, but my pride was still wounded and I fell back into playing hard ass.

"Thanks for waking me up." I said in a sarcastic voice.

Gina and Percy exchanged looks but said nothing. Still, I could tell that they had some sort of new understanding and my sarcasm had shocked them.

I guess I was looking for an argument, but they didn't bite. They said nothing at all and I watched as Gina turned and silently walked out of our cabin. I felt horrible. I wanted to apologize, but my pride was bruised and I felt betrayed. I felt like I had shared a wonderful, precious gift with them and then I was slapped in the face.

Percy came over and sat down on my cot. "I have something to tell you, Mike." he said. (There was that cold chill on my back again -- I could tell I was not going to like this). "He asked me to tell you not to bring up any more of the campers." Percy calmly told him.

I felt stunned, almost paralyzed in disbelief. "You mean he's quitting?" I asked.

"No, Mike. He doesn't want you to bring them up any more." Percy said with uneasiness in his voice." He asked Gina and me to do it for the rest of camp."

I felt dead. It was like all the life had gone out of me. I decided then that I was leaving camp as soon as possible. I hated him, and I hated the stupid camp, and I hated the instructors, and I hated all the campers, and I hated their lack of ability.

I was the best guitarist in camp and I knew it! Why were they all getting this special experience and I had to wait? I looked at Percy and I knew he saw the anger and disappointment in my eyes. He didn't say anything, he just looked away and then slowly walked out of the cabin. I was alone with my pain and anger once again. I was already thinking it was NO BIG DEAL. I had been walked out on before. I would survive without them and without the help of anyone else.

CHAPTER V: The Cold Heart

All that day I avoided everyone. I had decided I would go to lunch and then fake being sick. That would get me out of the ridiculous classes and allow me to pack up my stuff. I was leaving that night and I really didn't give a shit what happened after that. It felt strange dealing with my hurt and anger that afternoon.

I kept myself alone by acting aloof and cold towards everyone, but I was lonely and sad at the same time. I had seen some wonderful things in camp, but I had pretty much convinced myself it had all been an illusion and just one more lie.

It was funny how almost everyone sensed I was closing myself off and they stayed away from me. Even Gina and Percy only glanced over now and then from a distance. It was like being pulled out of time and taken someplace far, far away. The irony was, while I had never felt so alone before -- I also never felt so completely in touch with myself. I hated what I was doing, but I didn't know how in the world to deal with me.

CHAPTER VI: The Choice

After lunch, I told the camp counselors I was feeling sick. I said I didn't feel it was serious, but I did need to lay down for awhile. They asked me if I was sure it wasn't serious and I assured them it was not. I told them I had felt that way before and I just needed to rest.

Night came quickly. I didn't expect it, but the whole afternoon was unlike anything I had experienced before. I was very deep inside myself and it was like I was about to face an important decision or something. I couldn't quite put my finger on it, because earlier I had thought it would be cool to skip the camp. It would be like flipping all of them the finger, in a way.

Now that it was time to flip them all off, I felt unsure and scared. I began to wonder if I was doing the right thing. Being naturally stubborn, though, I decided it was too late to chicken out. I would leave when the Moon came up. That night there was a movie after dinner, so I would be alone for an extra three hours. Presuming everyone would be tired after it and fall asleep quickly, I would be able to sneak out around 11:30, or so.

I tossed and turned for a couple of hours before falling asleep. Then I was awakened by the sound of voices in the cabin. The light was off, so I couldn't see who it was, but I assumed the others had returned from watching the movie.

I played possum and said nothing while they prepared to go to bed. At one point, someone asked Percy if I was alright and Percy told them I was not to be disturbed. I laid in bed for about an hour, watching the full moon rise high into the sky. When I was sure that everyone was asleep, I slowly crept out of bed and walked out into the cool night.

The camp was poorly lit. I had to be careful not to stumble over anything again, but then again, the darkness also kept anyone else from seeing me leave. I quickly found the path and started walking back down to the main house and my car. It felt good to be leaving the camp.

I turned around and looked back toward the little valley with all the cramped cabins and the pain in the ass people. For a moment I felt sad as I thought about him -- James, I mean. It had been a special experience in my life, but I just couldn't deal with him now.

I could see the distant street lights of civilization. I actually took a deep breath when I realized I could see the main house where my car was parked and the cars on the interstate off in the distance. Feelings of freedom glossed over the old feelings of pain and frustration I had felt the last couple of days.

The walk down the hill to my car felt so good that I paid little attention to the path itself. Then it happened. My foot slid on something slick and I fell on my ass, sliding for several feet. I cursed out loud and then laughed at myself.

As I sat up, the laughter turned to a cold chill as I saw the pure white antique Fender Stratocaster at my feet. It was his guitar and I had stepped on it and then I fell. I looked all around, but no one was there. That didn't really surprise me, but it changed nothing. I was not going to turn back now.

I got up, brushing myself off and looking all around. Still seeing no one, I started to walk down the path again. I hadn't gone more than about three feet when I bumped smack into what felt like a tree and I hit the ground again. But it wasn't a tree -- it was him.

I sat there on the cold ground staring up at him. I couldn't see his face well, but I could see his eyes. They carried sadness in them that even the night could not hide.

"You lost, Mike?" he asked in a hushed voice.

"I'm leaving here." I said as I picked myself up and hurried to walk past him. I feared looking into his face. Something in his eyes grabbed at me and seemed to search out the parts of me I wanted to stay hidden.

"You're the best guitarist in this camp, Mike, but the saddest soul I have seen in a long while." he said as I passed by him.

"What's that supposed to mean?" I said as I turned and faced him in anger.

He slowly walked over to me and with his face only inches from mine, he looked deep into my eyes. I was scared to death. "See what I mean, Mike? You're so scared of yourself that you won't stay and face the truth." he said. "I can't stop you, but I can tell you this:

you will never find the music in your heart by running away."

"I'm not running away! I'm tired of your crap and all the waiting! I've brought you half the campers and I've seen the change in them. Don't you understand? I want to change, too!" I said in an angry tirade with tears streaming down my face.

The sadness that had been in his eyes turned to compassion and he placed a hand on my shoulder. "I will say this once more, Mike. You are the best guitarist in this camp. You are also heartless, cruel and an egotistical brat who hates himself. Even if you make it out in the world, you will destroy yourself." he said with a calmness that chilled me to the bone.

He turned to walk away and then he stopped and looked back. "The way I see it, you have a choice, Mike. You have a decision to make." he said. " I cannot interfere. I will help you find what you're looking for, but to find it, you'll have to stay at camp the remaining week."

"Why? There's nothing for me to do!" I said, as I wiped an escaping tear from my cheek.

"You and Gina and Percy will be bringing the others to see me. I only meant to bypass you for a day. I knew you were dealing with your own negative shit and I didn't want it affecting our work" he said with a crooked grin.

"You bastard!" I said, beaming again. "That's NOT how Percy said it, you know."

"He got it wrong, Mike. I love you. The universe loves you. Now you must decide if you will love yourself." He threw the words over his shoulder at me as he disappeared into the darkness.

I stood there undecided and cloudy in my thoughts. As I looked out over the valley I could see the main house where my car was parked -- the escape from myself that felt like some kind of freedom. When I thought about James and the camp I felt vulnerable and uneasy, but I also knew down deep that something was here that I needed to find and I needed to stay to discover it.

I was being pulled in two different directions. One way would let me feel safe, but only for a while and then the emptiness of my former life would creep back in and smother me. The other way felt like a death, but I wondered what I might find in that "death". I had been running away for a long time and I knew in my soul I could run no more. The decision was made and I started to walk back to the camp.

I was unusually aware as I walked quietly back into the campground. I felt alert and sharp. In my heart I felt coldness, perhaps a signal of a coming death and maybe a rebirth into something I could not yet understand.

I realized that my frustration and anger were gone, but I was not at peace. I had a new sense that I should allow things to naturally unfold, and somehow, I already knew that I had been fighting myself, even before James said so.

Quietly, I walked back into the cabin and put my stuff down on the floor by my cot. Looking around the cabin, I saw that everyone was fast asleep, I slowly slipped between my own sheets and took a deep breath. It was good to be back. It was good to know I faced myself and didn't run away. Yeah, I was scared, but I knew I would survive.

Just as I was feeling safe and about to fall asleep, a voice spoke to me out of the dark. "Glad you came back, man." said the familiar voice.

"Percy, is that you?" I said in a low voice, so I wouldn't wake the others.

"Yeah, Mike. I saw you leave. He said you would, but he also said there was a good chance you might come back. I'm glad you did. You know I don't have many friends. You are the first white dude I've had as a friend since grade school." Percy told me.

He made me smile. I thought to myself how beautiful it was that Percy had changed and opened up so much since coming to camp. I also thought how he and I were so much alike. We both had personal pain and we tried to hide it for so long, that it had become almost second nature to us. A familiar warmth crept into my heart.

"Thanks, Percy." I said.

"For what?" he asked.

"For having the courage to open your heart to me and talk about the pain you've carried inside. I've tried to hide mine behind the music and my pride, and I believe it's time to let the damn pride go." I told him.

"Yeah, I know. The guitar dude and I talked about that. He told me how it wasn't his playing that kept him from achieving success when he was alive, but his attitude. He told me and Gina to play for the love it brings to us first, and let the universe decide how big or famous we will be.

He said the magic is the love we discover in ourselves through the music. He told us that it creates some kind of feeling or energy that touches the hearts of other people. He said it was like being a pied piper, of sorts." Percy said.

I laid there on my cot thinking about what Percy said. I sure felt grateful for coming here and meeting him and the ghost who would not tell me his name. It was funny, but for the two weeks we were at camp, we all respected that privacy. I didn't feel compelled to pry it out of anybody else, and those who seemed to know more than me about him wouldn't share anymore with me, but it was okay.

At that point I yawned and told Percy goodnight. He did likewise and we both fell asleep fast.

CHAPTER VII: A New Day

That next morning was beautiful. A crystal sunlight shined through our window and a sense of electric excitement filled the cabin. We were all up at the same time and after yawning and stretching awhile we just started laughing.

When I first got here, I was shy, defensive, and very proud. Now I was open, vulnerable, and receptive to others. I really did love these guys -- they had helped me with that. Gina, and all the rest of them had played a large part in why I was feeling the way I did now. My anger and
frustration were almost gone. I felt loved and I felt a love for myself that I didn't realize was there. I was happy for the first time in my life, and I felt wonderful.

That last week went very fast, almost too fast. Percy, Gina, and I slowly and quietly brought the last of the campers to James each night so he could work his magic with them. We were a mystery to the older counselors. They knew something was going on, but figured it was just some crazy game we were playing.

Little by little, we all saw -- and especially heard -- that wonderful something which had crept into our music. We had more feeling, more heart and soul in how we played. We had learned to communicate our feelings into the music and we put the technical gimmicks on the back burner. We felt more in control as musicians and more honest as artists, because of it.

Finally, it was the last day of camp and it was my night to spend on the hill with James. I had enjoyed that week so much and spent so much spare time playing with my new awareness, that I was almost sorry it was coming to an end. A sense of sadness and loss filled me as I walked back to the cabin from dinner that night. We would all be gone tomorrow, and back into our own little worlds. I couldn't help but wonder if I would ever see James again.

That night, I lay on my cot fully awake for hours. I couldn't fall sleep, I was too excited. I used the time to relax and review all of my new feelings about everything. I could hardly wait for the moon to rise.

Suddenly, my eyes opened in horror! Shit, shit, shit! I had fallen asleep after all, and now it was morning! I had missed my meeting with James. Quickly, I threw on my clothes and with tears in my eyes I ran out the cabin door and sprinted up the hill. It was still early.

The sun hadn't peeked up over the horizon yet, maybe, just maybe ...

Confusion filled my thoughts and I had to fight back my anger for being so stupid and careless. My heart was pounding and I hoped he was still there and waiting.

About ten yards from the smoldering coals of the campfire, I slowed my pace and walked calmly into his camp. The campfire had been out for hours. A feeling of fear and anxiety came over me when I noticed an envelope posted to the tree where he used to lean his guitar. It was a plain white envelope with a letter inside.

> *Dear Mike,*
>
> *First of all relax. Take a deep breath and relax. All is well and perfect. You were expecting to meet me this last night, so I could give you something. The truth is, Mike, I never had anything to give you. I was merely a symbol to you and the others of the magic in the universe -- the impossible in a world of possibilities. I simply provided a stir for your imagination.*
>
> *You opened your heart Mike. You came back to face yourself and your fears. You trusted your feelings and played new music as you learned to love and accept yourself. You and the others carry the magic inside of you and you access it whenever you love and accept yourself as you are.*
>
> *Finally Mike, it doesn't matter who I am, but rather, who you become. I have helped you to see the power of love inside you. Now it is up to you to share that love with the world. Believe me Mike, the love will guide you to everything in its proper time.*
>
> *Stay Free,*
> *Jimi*

A feeling of deep and overwhelming gratitude filled me as I hugged myself and fell to my knees sobbing. I was not hurting, just fully aware of the message and intent of the letter and releasing the many years of pain, anger and guilt.

I had hidden the music all those years under my own garbage. Nobody had kept it from me, except me. I made a vow to myself that morning, never to blame anything or anyone again for my life. I'd take full responsibility for my thoughts and feelings and then dedicate myself to the love I found inside myself.

As I walked back down to the cabin, a sense of profound peace filled my whole being. It was like I'd purged myself of a whole lifetime of sorrow and pain.

Percy, Gina and the others met me outside my cabin. They'd packed up my few belongings. A peaceful stillness filled the spot outside the cabin where we stood looking at each other. We were equals and so alive.

After a few minutes, we all hugged. Warm tears filled our eyes as we realized that a special time in our lives was now over. We wished each other luck and exchanged phone numbers. Gina promised we would talk often.

I picked up my stuff and holding Gina's hand we all walked together to the path that would take us back to our own realities. No one said much on the way back. The embracing and the tears had spoken for themselves, back at the cabin, and everything important had already been said. Each one of us knew we were forever changed and that life would be more real from then on.

I said my final goodbyes and got into my car to drive back down the long dirt road to the interstate. Feeling sad and a little melancholy, I turned on the radio and picked up one of the local rock stations. It was odd how much more I felt in tune with the music. I could now sense the difference between music that was played just to make music and the music created by true artists who put their hearts and souls into it. This was the music that flowed through them that Jimi had taught us about.

I turned the radio's knob again through some static and stopped on a strong oldies station that was playing some 60's stuff.   As I was listening to a guitarist, I found myself moving to the music in my seat. It was brilliant and it compelled me to feel the music. I couldn't control myself. This guy was putting these powerful feelings into each note on his guitar.

Then the DJ broke in and said that the name of the song was "Purple Haze." It was done by a man named Jimi Hendrix. I had heard a lot about him, but I had never really listened to his music before. I guess I had never understood till then what he had felt.

Just then, I glanced in my rear view mirror and that's when I saw his face. I turned to see if he was in the back seat. He was gone. I smiled to myself and, as I drove onto the interstate, I wondered if James Marshall had known Jimi Hendrix in his life.   Was it only a coincidence that James Marshall had signed my letter, "Jimi"?   Oh well ... I'm sure they would have gotten along very well, had they known each other ...

Epilogue:

Thank you for taking the time to read my book. I hope you enjoyed the three stories as much as I enjoyed writing them.

I have several other books finished and they will be published during the next year. The working titles are:

"Awareness: The Magic Within"

"The Magic of Love and Intimacy"

"The Book of Whispers I & II"

"The Poetry of Awareness and Awakening"

"The Astrology of Awareness"

Namaste!

Robert

www.ingramcontent.com/pod-product-compliance
Lightning Source LLC
Chambersburg PA
CBHW051502170626
46811CB00002B/601